"Why do you keep running away from me?"

Casey was startled by Ivo's question, especially when he added, "Twice now you've run from me like a startled rabbit. Why?"

"Possibly because you're very pushy," Casey answered crossly. "And also very nosy. What were you doing last night—spying on me?"

"Women always try to change the subject when they have something to hide," Ivo observed. "I know enough about women to know whether they're, shall we say, interested in me."

"Well I'm not, if that's what you're getting at," Casey said swiftly.

"Aren't you? Perhaps I used the wrong word, then. Perhaps I should have said immune. Because you're certainly not immune to me, are you, Casey?"

SALLY WENTWORTH began her publishing career at a Fleet Street newspaper in London, where she thrived in the hectic atmosphere. After her marriage, she and her husband moved to rural Hertfordshire, where Sally had been raised. Although she worked for the publisher of a group of magazines, the day soon came when her own writing claimed her energy and time.

Books by Sally Wentworth

HARLEQUIN PRESENTS
 814—THE WINGS OF LOVE
 837—FATAL DECEPTION
 862—THE HAWK OF VENICE
 926—THE KISSING GAME
 974—CAGE OF ICE
 997—TIGER IN HIS LAIR
1046—PASSIONATE REVENGE
1094—DISHONOURABLE INTENTIONS
1109—ULTIMATUM
1142—MISTAKEN WEDDING
1165—SATAN'S ISLAND
1197—DRIVING FORCE
1220—THE DEVIL'S SHADOW
1237—STRANGE ENCOUNTER
1278—WISH ON THE MOON
1309—ECHOES OF THE PAST

HARLEQUIN ROMANCE
2262—LIBERATED LADY
2310—THE ICE MAIDEN
2361—GARDEN OF THORNS

SALLY
WENTWORTH

fire island

Harlequin Books

TORONTO • NEW YORK • LONDON
AMSTERDAM • PARIS • SYDNEY • HAMBURG
STOCKHOLM • ATHENS • TOKYO • MILAN

Harlequin Presents first edition January 1991
ISBN 0-373-11334-X

Original hardcover edition published in 1989
by Mills & Boon Limited

CHAPTER ONE

'GREAT news! I think we've hooked Vulcan Enterprises.' Steve came bursting into Casey's office with a big grin lighting his face.

'Really? That's great.' Casey Grant smiled at her partner. 'Have they written to you?'

'No, one of their directors has just phoned and asked to make an appointment to discuss it further. So it looks as if all that homework we did on the company has paid off.'

'Who called you—their PR man?'

Steve consulted the sheet of paper he was holding in his hand. 'No, it was one of their directors— another good sign. His name is Ivo Maine, and I gather he's in charge of promotions, sales, advertising, all that side of the company. And if we can get him to place just one contract with us . . .'

'Then we'll have a foot in the door, and with a corporation that big, who knows what it might lead to?' Casey finished for him. 'Steve, that's great. You must have really sold us to them. Did you meet this Ivo Maine?'

'Briefly, I think. But I was introduced to several people while I was there for my meeting with the PR man. I seem to remember that Maine was quite young to hold that high a position in the company.'

Casey raised her eyebrows. 'Nepotism, do you think?'

'Hard to say. He might be related to the owners, of course, but if he isn't he must be pretty good. I'll try and find out some more about him before you see him.'

'Have you made an appointment?'

'Yes, you're to go and see him on Thursday at ten-thirty. I take it that's OK?'

'Of course. This could lead to a nice fat contract for us, Steve. You've done well.'

He smiled, pleased with her praise. 'Well, now it's up to you to convince him that we can give Vulcan Enterprises the standard of artwork that they want.'

They talked over the good news for a while until Steve went back to his own office, promising to find out as much as he could about Ivo Maine before Casey went to see him. She turned back to her own work, first consulting her diary to make sure that she would have the whole of Thursday free to devote to the meeting at Vulcan Enterprises. After a few moments' thought, she decided to cancel a lunch date she had for that day just in case the meeting went on longer than she expected; it wouldn't do to have to excuse herself before any decisions had been made. Putting her head out of the door, Casey asked their shared secretary, Heather, to call the supplier she had intended to lunch with on Thursday and ask him to re-schedule the appointment. Then she returned to the work she had been doing earlier, the artwork for the boxes for a new range of frozen foods for one of their best customers.

Her thoughts, though, drifted away to the coming interview with Vulcan. She was pleased that Steve had gained an entry there, and even more pleased that he was now entirely confident of her abilities to push the sale through alone. There had been a time, when she had first taken over the partnership after Mike had died, when Steve had insisted on coming along with her to every meeting and discussion, anxiously overseeing every detail in case she put the company that he and Mike had so lovingly and laboriously built up into jeopardy. But gradually, over the ensuing two and a half years, Steve had come to rely on Casey more and more, and she could now regard herself as a true partner in Decart, their art and design consultancy.

When Thursday came, Casey set off in good time for her appointment with Vulcan Enterprises. As the director of a company that dealt with colour and design, she felt justified in getting away from the typical businesswoman image of smart, dark-coloured suits, instead wearing a chic lemon coat over a lemon print dress. Not very practical for damp London streets, perhaps, especially the matching high-heeled shoes, but they made Casey feel good, ready to meet the executive she wanted to do business with. And, from what they had managed to find out about him, Ivo Maine sounded as if he might be an exacting potential client.

Steve had been in touch with several contacts: existing customers, friends in the City, those kind of people, to find out as much as he could about Maine before Casey went to see him, and the general opinion was surprisingly similar from everyone who knew him: that he was brilliant at his job but had no time for the foolish or inefficient. Rather an intimidating prospect, Casey thought, as the taxi carried her through the snarled streets to the city. But she had faced men who had tried to intimidate her before, probably because they had thought it would be easy to browbeat a woman, and they had soon been enlightened. Some, too, had tried the old male chauvinist approach, paying her unnecessary compliments and trying to undermine her resolve by flattery, but they had been even more speedily disillusioned. Raised eyebrows over a steady look from her cool green eyes, and a calm request to get back to business, had deflated all but the most pig-headed of MCPs.

They were in the city now, the square mile at the heart of London where all the major companies had their offices in the stately old buildings or new concrete and glass towers, all crowded together in this small area bounded by the river and the remnants of the ancient city walls. The taxi turned into Threadneedle Street and went past the Bank of England. Not far to go now. Casey glanced at her watch and saw that it was nearly ten-fifteen. Good, she had timed it just right. Even if there was a hold-up she could get out and walk from here. She sat back for the last part of the journey with a small smile, remembering that she hadn't always been so punctual; but then, she hadn't always been so cool and businesslike either. It was something she had had to learn when she went into partnership with Steve. Before that she had always relied on Mike; he had been the punctual one, the successful career man with an assured future. But his death had changed everything, and from it, out of necessity, she had learnt strength and efficiency.

The taxi drew up in front of an imposing building in a much quieter side street off Cornhill. Carrying her large briefcase, Casey went to the entrance and saw that nearly the whole building was taken up by Vulcan Enterprises. Crossing to the reception desk, she gave her name to the man there and waited while he phoned through.

'If you could go up to the third floor, please, madam. Mr Maine's office is straight ahead of you as you come out of the lift.'

Casey thanked him and looked about her as she crossed to the lift. It was certainly impressive; there was an air of quiet opulence about the place, both inside and out, and luckily someone had had the good sense not to sacrifice old wooden panelling and tall double doors to modern partitions and artificial plants. The lift was discreetly hidden away in a corner and they had kept the magnificent sweeping staircase that curved to the next floor and then up towards the large rectangular skylight set into the roof, which gave little light on this dull February day.

There was thick carpet on the floor as Casey stepped out at the third floor. Presumably the carpet got thicker the higher up the executive list you were, she thought rather cynically. She walked the short way down the corridor to Ivo Maine's door, and found that he was guarded by a middle-aged dragon with sculptured hair, who was wearing a tailored suit. Casey gave her name again and was asked to take a seat. She was kept waiting for nearly twenty minutes, which didn't please her, but it gave her another opportunity to look around and decide what kind of artwork to recommend to such a staid and conservative company.

A buzzer sounded on the dragon's desk and she stood up. 'Mr Maine will see you now.' She walked towards the far door but, before opening it, said, 'Is it Miss or Mrs Grant?'

'Ms,' Casey responded, having been kept waiting long enough to be unhelpful.

She received a sniff and a frown in reply before the secretary opened the door and announced, 'Casey Grant to see you, Mr Maine.'

The office was exactly as Casey had expected it to be: large, traditionally furnished and luxurious, and at first glance Ivo Maine, who was standing with his back to her as he read a VDU screen, seemed to be what she'd expected as well, for he was wearing the same kind of dark, well-cut business-suit that most City men wore. But then he finished reading and swung round to face her, and all Casey's preconceived ideas did a lightning change.

Her first impression was of strength and power; he was very tall, about six foot three, she guessed, and he looked lean and athletic, not like a man who spent most of his life at a desk. But his strength wasn't solely physical, the main part of it seemed to come from within and showed in the bright keenness of his look as his grey eyes summed her up, the firmness of his jaw, and the masculine self-confidence as his lips twisted into a thin smile.

'Good morning. Your colleague neglected to tell me that you were a woman; such a convenient anonymity—a unisex name.'

A superpig, Casey thought. But at least he came right out with it even if he did add a snide remark. But she had learnt how to stand up for herself in a tough school, and so said in a deceptively sweet voice, 'Would it have made any difference?'

He gave her a keen glance. 'Not if you know your job.'

'Then my sex hardly matters, does it?' she answered shortly. 'Shall we get down to business, Mr Maine? I'm sure you must be a *very* busy man.' And she laid a faint emphasis on the 'very', because he'd kept her waiting so long and hadn't bothered to apologise.

But he'd caught the message all right; his left eyebrow, the one with the slight arch in it, rose. 'By all means. I'm afraid I've already wasted some of your very valuable time by keeping you waiting. Unfortunately I received a very important Fax message that had to be dealt with immediately; such a shame our New York office didn't realise that I had an appointment with you,' he said in gently mocking irony.

Realising that she had met her match, Casey said stiffly, 'I've brought along some samples of the kind of work we think you might be interested in for your calendar, if you'd care to look at them. But perhaps you already have some ideas of your own.'

She balanced her briefcase on the edge of his desk, but Maine gestured towards the other end of his office where there was a maroon leather chesterfield and some other chairs grouped round a large coffee-table. 'Shall we sit over there?'

Taking care to choose a chair rather than the settee, Casey sat down, took from her case a batch of previous calendars that Decart had designed and laid them on the table. Maine gave them a cursory glance, but didn't even bother to pick them up.

Leaning back in the chesterfield, his arm along the back, he said, 'I thought I made it plain to your colleague that I wanted something completely original.'

Straightening up, Casey gave him a direct look. 'Yes, so my *partner* told me. But originality costs money,' she said bluntly. 'I should have to study the products you wish to advertise in depth, and probably do a great deal of research to come up with something that hasn't been done before. And that will take time, too. If you want the calendar to come out in time for this Christmas, we will have to start work at once,' she warned.

'But it can be done?'

'Anything can be done, given sufficient backing and drive,' Casey answered.

'Well, I'm willing to supply the backing if I'm convinced that you can give me what I want: an eye-catching calendar that will not only advertise our products but be a conversation piece in itself. Another Pirelli collector's item, if you like.'

Wow! You don't want much, Casey thought, but her eyes gleamed with enthusiasm at the challenge it represented. It was the sort of opening she and Steve had been looking for. If they could pull this off, their name would be made and the orders would come rolling in thick and fast.

She glanced up to find Ivo Maine's eyes on her face. 'Can you do it?' he demanded.

'Certainly. Perhaps you could give me a summary of the products you want to advertise? And I should like as much literature as you have available so that I can really study them. And if you've had any market research reports done on any of the products, that would be a help too. Anything you have, in fact,' she said with mounting eagerness.

Maine gave a small smile. 'I've already had my secretary put together a file for you. She'll give it to you when you go. But, briefly, we apply the technology of heat to create various products. Heat-resistant paint, for example.'

'Oh, I see. That's why you're called Vulcan Enterprises—Vulcan is the god of fire.'

'Quite so,' Maine said drily.

He went on to describe the various products manufactured by the companies under the Vulcan umbrella, and Casey listened keenly. But she watched him, too, observing the way he stressed a point with his hands—long, eloquent hands with manicured nails that didn't look as if they had ever done a menial task. He wore a ring on his right hand and there were gold links in the cuffs of his unbelievably white shirt, a gold Rolex watch on his wrist; but they weren't ostentatious, for use more than for display. His suit, too, was of excellent quality and cut, and he wore a tie of discreet diagonal stripes that Casey guessed must be that of some old public school or perhaps an army regiment. She wasn't into men's clothes nowadays, but could recognise quality when she saw it.

So, putting everything together, this definitely put Ivo Maine into the privileged class. She guessed a very upper-middle-class background of prep school, followed by Eton or Harrow and then one of the older universities, Oxford probably. Perhaps, then, a few years as an officer in the army to teach him command, and then into this job with a relative pulling a few strings to get him in at a high level.

Raising her eyes, Casey found that he was watching her as he finished speaking, again with that slightly twisted smile. She had the uncanny feeling that he knew what she was thinking, and this was borne out when he said, 'Cynicism isn't becoming in a female.'

Casey caught her breath but refused to be intimidated. 'Nor is sarcasm in a male,' she retorted.

To her surprise he looked amused. 'Now, is that any way to speak to a potential customer?'

'Is that any way to speak to someone who can provide you with the expertise you require to advertise your products?' Casey countered.

This time he laughed outright, and she realised he preferred this no-nonsense approach, which was lucky because somehow he wasn't the kind of man she could put on an act for, even to gain an order like this. Not that she had it definitely yet.

Glancing at his watch, Maine stood up. 'Why don't we finish discussing this over lunch? And you can tell me what experience you've had in producing the kind of thing we want.'

He was already half-way to the door, but Casey didn't scramble to collect her sample calendars and join him, instead taking her time and zipping up her briefcase before she stood up and said, 'Thank you, as a matter of fact I *am* free for lunch.'

She walked over to the door which he was holding open for her and saw that there was amused mockery in his grey eyes. 'I was sure you would be,' he said mendaciously. He received a fiery glance from her green eyes that deepened his amusement. 'By the way, is it Miss or Mrs Grant?'

'It's Ms,' his secretary informed him as she came round her desk. 'I already asked her.' And she held out a bulky folder. 'The literature you wanted.'

'Thank you, Marilyn; I should have known.' He led the way out to the lift and pressed the button, then turned and raised an enquiring eyebrow when he saw the laughter in Casey's face. She shook her head, trying to hide it, but he guessed anyway. 'A rose by any other name,' he quoted softly.

Casey laughed openly. 'But Marilyn! I thought people were supposed to live up to their names.'

'But perhaps rebels try to do the opposite. Perhaps Marilyns are made by nature to be like my secretary and it was Marilyn Monroe who rebelled.'

'Ah, I see—an example of lateral thinking,' Casey said with a smile.

The lift came and they got in. 'We have a very good dining-room in the building,' Maine remarked, 'so I hope you don't mind if we eat here. It's so much more convenient than booking a restaurant.'

And so much cheaper too. Casey suddenly realised where her thoughts were heading and a small frown creased her brows; maybe Maine was right, maybe she *was* becoming cynical. It troubled her a little because she had tried so hard not to become bitter, although she'd had cause enough, heaven knew. She would just have to try harder, she resolved. And after all, Ivo Maine didn't have to take her to lunch at all; really it should be the other way round—as a potential customer she should be treating him. She tried to remember whether Steve had taken him out for a meal, but couldn't recall her partner having mentioned it.

The dining-room was on the ground floor and was very large. In the centre was a big oval table around which several men were already sitting; the directors' table presumably, and round the edges of the room were smaller tables for two or four people. Maine led her to one with only two seats, helped her to take off her coat and then held a chair for her to sit down.

'Now, what would you like to drink?' he asked.

'Just Perrier water, please.'

He gave a small grin. 'Ah, you're like policemen, are you? Never drink on duty.'

'I drink socially,' Casey answered rather defensively.

'But you obviously don't feel that this is a social occasion.'

'Should one mix business with pleasure?' she asked lightly.

'Why not, if it's feasible? I see no harm in it as long as one gets one's priorities right.'

Which rather depended on which became the more important, the business or the pleasure, Casey thought. She glanced up and found Maine looking at her with that slightly amused expression again, and she had the uncomfortable feeling that he knew exactly what she was thinking. It occurred to her that he wouldn't have looked at a man like that, and her chin came up defiantly. 'Personally I prefer to keep the two completely separate.'

'Really? Then you're evidently a dedicated career woman. One of the new breed that's taking over the City and industry,' he intoned mockingly.

Casey gave him a level look from her cool, green eyes. 'And one which you obviously don't care for.'

'Did I give that impression?' He pretended to be surprised. 'On the contrary, I have great admiration for career women—as long as they don't become obsessive about it, of course.' His eyes ran over her dress and he said, 'At least you don't dress in drab colours like most of them seem to.'

He said it with a slightly raised eyebrow, and Casey felt compelled to say, 'I suppose that's because colour is my business. And I think colour is psychologically important too.'

'You mean if you wear bright colours it makes you feel good and vice versa?'

'In its simplest version, yes,' Casey admitted.

A waitress came up with the menus and Maine said casually, 'You must tell me more about it some time. What would you like to eat, M——' He frowned. 'I can't keep calling you Ms; it sounds like a female bumble-bee. Do you mind if I call you Casey?'

'Not at all,' she answered politely.

'And I'm Ivo, of course.'

She nodded and bent her head to study the menu. They certainly did themselves well at Vulcan; the dishes were as good as in a restaurant, even if there wasn't quite such a wide choice. Avoiding the more exotic dishes, Casey settled for a modest salad. That brought another glance at her already very slim figure.

'You're obviously not very hungry,' he commented.

'No, Mr Maine, you said . . .'

'Ivo,' he corrected.

'You said that you wanted to know what experience I've had. Well, I have an arts degree and I worked for a very well-known advertising agency for several years before I joined Decart.'

She was about to continue, but Ivo said, 'Did you join them as a partner? Were you in at the start of the company?'

Casey shook her head. 'I only worked for them on a part-time basis when they first started. But then— then one of the partners died and I went to work for the company full-time and eventually took over the partnership.'

'I see. Well, Decart are certainly gaining a very high reputation, so I imagine you deserved your partnership.'

'Thank you.' Deciding to be bold, Casey said, 'Does that mean that you're going to give us your order for the calendar, Mr . . . Ivo?'

He smiled. 'No, I'm not.'

Casey's face tightened as she struggled to hide her disappointment. Steve would never forgive her for this after all the hard work he'd put into trying to get this contract. Ivo was still smiling at her, damn him! He must have decided right at the beginning that he wasn't going to do business with her, but had made up his mind to let her go on hoping. 'Would you mind telling me why not?' she asked shortly, trying hard to keep the chagrin out of her voice.

Their food came and he didn't answer until the waitress had gone. He looked at her directly then, and recognised the flare of angry disappointment in her eyes.

'I suppose I'd better tell you, or you'll get the most terrible indigestion by trying to eat and suppress your temper at the same time.' But he seemed in no hurry, tilting his head to one side as he looked at her and saying, 'I wonder why it is that all redheads have flaming tempers to go with it?'

'My hair isn't red. Why aren't you going to give us the contract?'

'Red-gold, then. I am not going to give you a contract for the calendar, but I am going to give you the go-ahead to do the research for it and to come up with some ideas. When I see those, then I'll decide about the final contract.'

Casey stared at him for a moment, quite taken aback, but then recovered and said quickly, 'And expenses?'

'How much do you think they will be?'

'Your company deals with heat technology; so it could be that the calendar will need to be set in a hot, exotic setting. I might have to go abroad to find a suitable background.'

Ivo nodded. 'That's no more than I expected. We'll pay all reasonable expenses—and you will of course have that in writing,' he added as he saw her open her mouth to speak. 'I'll have Marilyn type out an agreement and send it to you. But I shall want you to give this your full attention so that we can go ahead as soon as possible,' he warned.

'Of course. Thank you,' Casey said rather inadequately.

She began to eat, realising that she would have to revise her first opinion of her companion. When he had said he wouldn't give her the contract she had been disappointed, but not really surprised. All along, in the back of her mind, she had felt that he wasn't taking her seriously just because she happened to be female, that he was even enjoying playing a cat-and-mouse game with her. The mocking way he had spoken to her certainly seemed to emphasise that. But she hadn't been entirely sure. That emphatic 'No, I'm not,' had seemed to clinch it, but then he had really surprised her by telling her to go ahead with the research. So what was she supposed to make of him now?

Ivo refilled her glass with Perrier water and she glanced up at him. He smiled at her and Casey found herself smiling back, able to relax now that her anxiety about the order had been allayed. 'Have you been with Vulcan long?' she asked.

'About five years.'

He didn't elaborate, so she didn't press him to go on, but she began to feel curious about him. She guessed that he was only about thirty-two or thirty-three; as Steve had said, very young to be in such a high position in a large company. They had surmised that Ivo probably had connections within Vulcan which had helped him to gain his present position, but now Casey wondered if he hadn't got there on his own merit. He certainly seemed intelligent and confident enough. And now that the business part of their meeting was over, she began to feel curious about him as a man, too. He was knowledgeable about women; she was quite sure of that, had been from the start. It was the sort of thing a woman always instinctively knew about a man. And he had proved it from the way that he could guess what she was thinking. Casey wondered if he was married and sneaked a look at his left hand, but he wore no rings.

'Do you go to art exhibitions much?' he asked her, and Casey wrenched her mind away from useless surmise.

'When I have the time. Not as often as I'd like to, of course. But in some ways that's a good thing because it means we're busy at Decart.'

'It sounds as if you work long hours,' Ivo commented.

'When necessary,' Casey agreed.

'Don't you find that interferes with your home and family commitments?'

'No,' Casey answered positively. 'This is extremely good food. You must have a very experienced chef.'

Ivo's eyes lingered on her set face for a moment, but he accepted the change of subject. 'Yes, a woman as a matter of fact. We were lucky to get her; she was thinking of starting her own restaurant, but was persuaded to come and work for us instead, so long as she had the choice of menu.'

They went on to talk of other things and the time passed quickly. Sometimes they touched on work, but mostly they discussed impartial subjects, so that Casey felt more and more at ease and could laugh and be as bright and witty as she would be among her friends and colleagues. Her naturalness brought an answering response from Ivo, and she found to her surprise that she was beginning to like him. He gave her his undivided attention, his eyes fixed on her when she was speaking, making her feel that her views were of importance to him, and he didn't talk down to her when he answered. Casey almost felt as if she had passed some kind of test and that he now accepted her as an equal—in business at least. But she couldn't help wondering how he would have treated her if she'd met him socially; would he have flirted with her, using his undoubted charm and good looks to attract her? she wondered. And would she have been interested?

That thought brought her up short; not because of who she was thinking about, but because the thought had come to her at all. She hadn't thought of a man like that in years. It frightened her, made her feel mixed up and angry inside. Quickly, now, she finished her coffee and said rather abruptly, 'It was very kind of you to give me lunch, but if you're sure that there's nothing else, then I think I'd better be getting back to the office. I want to clear my desk as soon as possible so that I can start on the research for your project.'

Ivo smiled and stood up. 'Of course. Here, let me help you with your coat.' He did so, and waited until Casey had picked up her bag and briefcase, then held out his hand to her. 'Goodbye, Casey, I've enjoyed our lunch. And I look forward to working with you.'

He shook her hand, his grip firm, then walked with her to the main door where he waited until the doorman showed her out. Out on the pavement, Casey glanced back for a moment and saw him still watching her. He raised his hand in a gesture of farewell, and she gave him one of her sudden smiles that transformed her face, lighting her features into beauty. Then she turned and raised her hand to attract a taxi that was cruising along the street.

Her first thought when she was alone was that Steve would be pleased with the outcome of her interview—even if she hadn't got a signed contract she had the next best thing, because she was quite sure that she could come up with some ideas that Ivo would like. Ivo—her mind went back to him and she wondered again if he was married. Probably, most good-looking, go-ahead men got snapped up early because their potential was easily recognisable. Any girl aiming to have a very well-feathered nest would be on the look-out for a man of his type. But no, Casey suddenly felt that she was wrong, there was something about him that made her feel that he was still free. She smiled a little, remembering how unfavourable her first impression had been, and how swiftly it had been revised. It would be pleasant to meet him again, she thought, and again was amazed that she should feel like that. Either Ivo Maine was a much more magnetic man than she'd realised, or she was beginning to recover from Mike's death, as everyone had prophesied she would. 'Time is a great healer.' She could hear the voices now, trying to comfort her. And how she had hated to hear them, had wanted those people to feel the hurt that she was experiencing so that they wouldn't force upon her their inane, useless clichés.

Her eyes grew dark with remembered pain, which was still there when she arrived back at the office and went up to see Steve. He took one look at her face and said heavily, 'You didn't get the contract.'

For a moment she was tempted to tease him, but shook off her blue mood and gave him a big smile, 'Oh, ye of little faith. Of course I got it—or at least the next best thing. Maine is putting an agreement in the post for us to go ahead with the research, and if he likes our ideas then the contract's ours.'

'Ya-hoo!' Steve picked her up and swung her round. 'You doll. I was beginning to be afraid you hadn't got the contract and were too scared to come back and tell me, you've been gone so long.'

'No, I was having lunch with Ivo. How about that? *And* he's promised to meet all our expenses if I have to go abroad to find a good background.'

'Ivo, is it? I didn't get that far with him. He obviously has an eye for a beautiful girl.' He grinned and held up his hands defensively as she glared at him. 'OK, don't slaughter me, I'm sure it was your brain and expertise that hooked him,' he teased. 'Did he come up with any ideas himself? These executives usually think they know how to design the thing better than we do.'

'No, he didn't even look at the examples I took with me. He's leaving it all to me. And if he's going to get the calendar in time for this Christmas I'd better go and get to work,' Casey told him, already half-way to the door.

During the afternoon Casey cleared as much work as she could, staying on at the office long after Steve had left. He put his head in the door to say goodnight, but didn't attempt to persuade her to go home; he had learnt the hard way that it was of no use, that she would rather stay on and work than go home to an empty house. It was after eight-thirty when Casey finally left, but even then she carried home several reference books and the file that Ivo had given her. As soon as she'd eaten her microwaved ready-meal, Casey settled down in a chair with a notepad beside her to try and come up with some ideas for Vulcan's calendar.

Their products and technology seemed to cover a wide range, everything from solar power to the application of heat in chemistry to produce synthetic materials. She made notes as she read, as always becoming completely absorbed in the current project, and it was the early hours before she at last went up to bed. Not that this was at all unusual; she had got into the habit of going to bed late and getting up early, not because she didn't need the sleep but because it made the nights a whole lot shorter to get through.

The next morning she was already sitting at her desk when Steve came in. It was their custom to have a coffee together before the rest of the staff arrived, when they would discuss the progress of work in hand and decide on the programme for themselves and the staff.

'You look pleased with yourself,' Steve commented.

Casey smiled. 'I was going through the material that Ivo Maine gave me at home last night, and I think I've got the beginnings of an idea.'

'How many times have I told you that you don't need to take work home?' Steve said mechanically, knowing that it would be ignored. 'You should go out and enjoy yourself more. What was the idea?'

She threw him an affectionate look. 'I'll tell you when I have something definite. Let me know when the agreement from Vulcan's arrives, will you? I want to see exactly what Ivo Maine is offering.'

Going into her office, Casey picked up the big dictionary and looked up Vulcan. 'The god of fire and metal-working,' she read. 'Volcanic...a blacksmith...to treat with sulphur.' And lastly, 'Vulcan's badge, a cuckold's horns.' Which made her grin.

Pensively she sat down at her desk and swivelled the chair round until she was looking out of the window at the heavy grey sky. It was cold today and looked as if it might snow. She shivered and reached for the well-thumbed world atlas on the shelf behind her. She studied it until Heather came in with the post, the letter from Ivo Maine at the top of the pile.

'Steve has already seen Vulcan's letter and he says it's fine,' Heather told her.

'OK. Thanks.' Casey picked up the letter and read it through, noting Ivo's strong, almost arrogant signature at the end. It gave a spending limit that was generous to say the least. On the strength of it, Casey put on her coat and went round to the local library where she headed for the geographical section. She spent some time there, studying various illustrated travel guides and reading up on several places that interested her. At the end of a couple of hours she sat back with a satisfied smile, then hurried back to the office and caught Steve just as he was leaving to go to the nearest pub for lunch.

He looked at her bright face and said, 'I take it you're ready to tell me your idea now? Come on, then, you can tell me over a pint at the pub.'

They walked across to the King's Head and sat at the table by the window, where Steve had always sat with Mike when he was alive. Casey had occasionally joined them then, but after Mike died Steve had had to come here alone for quite some time before she had found the courage to come with him again. They said hello to the other regulars, fellow businessmen from other small firms in the area mostly, just a few women standing out among so many men. It was Steve's turn to pay today; they took it in turns, with no silliness about him paying because she was a woman. Theirs was an equal partnership in every way, Casey had always insisted on that.

'Well, what's the idea?' He came back with their drinks and sat down opposite her.

'Well, I thought Vulcan—volcano, right? Why not have a setting where there has been a volcanic eruption or even a still active volcano? Heat in its most violent form. And some of the rock formations they leave behind are really fantastic. They would make a great background for the models. And we could bring the god of fire into it, too.' She went on enthusiastically and Steve nodded, sharing her excitement.

'You're right, it's a great idea. Where are you thinking of going—to Italy, or Mount Etna, somewhere like that?'

'Possibly, but it's a bit obvious. I thought I'd go to the Canary Islands first; I've been looking at photographs of them in the library, and I think there are definite possibilities there.'

'And also a fantastic climate,' Steve said drily. 'Fancy getting an assignment like that in the depths of winter. You have all the luck.'

Casey looked away. 'Yes, don't I?' she agreed stiltedly.

Steve glanced up at her tone and gave a groan. 'Lord, Casey, I'm sorry. I didn't think.'

Putting out her hand to touch his, she smiled and said, 'Why should you, for heaven's sake?' And quickly changed the subject. 'When can I go and take a look at the islands? I really ought to go as soon as possible.'

They talked it over some more, with the result that Casey found herself on a plane only a couple of days later. She went first to Tenerife, hiring a car and driving herself all round the island, stopping to take lots of photographs, and often walking off the beaten track if she thought an area might be of use. From Tenerife she took a boat across to the neighbouring islands of Gran Canaria, Fuerteventura and Lanzarote. She stayed longest at the latter and here took more detailed photographs, as well as making lots of sketches. Then, satisfied that she'd found what she wanted, she flew back to England to find a thick layer of snow everywhere, which somehow came as a surprise after the warm sunshine of the Canaries.

She had been away for about a week, and spent another few days perfecting her ideas and sketches before she rang to make another appointment with Ivo Maine.

He agreed to see her the following day, and Casey went along in a mood of buoyant optimism, sure in her mind that her ideas were good and would interest him, and feeling an almost forgotten stirring of pleasure at the thought of seeing him again.

Ivo came forward with a smile to greet her, and helped her off with her coat, a red one this time. 'I can see by your face that you think you've come up with some good ideas,' he commented. 'Come and sit down and tell me all about them.'

He led the way over to the settee and this time Casey sat beside him. 'I've been over to the Canary Islands,' she told him. 'To Lanzarote mostly. I don't know if you've ever been there?' She looked at him enquiringly, but Ivo shook his head. 'It's the most fantastic place. Completely volcanic, so that even the earth is black or red. And there are the most weird and wonderful rock formations caused by the molten lava. I went all over the island and I came up with these ideas.'

Reaching down, Casey untied the big portfolio she'd brought with her and took out a series of large composite pictures she'd made up by using blown-up photographs as the background with superimposed sketches added. She went to explain how she'd come by her idea, but Ivo held up his hand to stop her. 'No, let the pictures speak for themselves.'

He studied them one by one, making no comments or criticisms, while Casey waited in growing suspense. She watched his face, trying to see his reaction, but he gave nothing away, merely flicking a glance at her once or twice and giving a small smile, which was no help or comfort at all. At last he straightened up and stacked the pictures into a neat pile, then he turned to look at her—and gave a big grin!

'They're brilliant,' he told her. 'I'm sure we're on to a winner. I'll have a contract drawn up for you straight away so that you can go ahead immediately. Now, as to the models you'll want; how many do you think you'll need?'

'Not more than three girls and one man. We can make them look different with wigs and make-up if necessary. But we'll need more than just the models, you know. There will be quite a team of people, and they'll need a caravan or coach or something to transport them and their equipment, as well as accommodation on the island. As a matter of fact, I made enquiries about accommodation while I was in Lanzarote, and I think the best thing would be for the whole team to stay at one of the new holiday developments.' She realised that Ivo was grinning at her and she came to a stop.

'You were obviously pretty sure that my answer would be favourable,' he commented.

Casey flushed a little. 'I hoped you'd be pleased, yes. And I thought that if I made enquiries while I was actually on the island it would save time—and money.'

'Very efficient. And I'm quite happy to leave all those arrangements in your hands. But we were speaking about the models.' He paused, and something in his tone made Casey suddenly feel wary. 'I'm sure there are a great many to choose from, but there is one in particular I'd like you to use. Her name is Lucy Grainger.'

Casey frowned, already more than half-afraid of what was coming. 'I don't think I've heard of her; does she work in England?'

'I'm sure you haven't heard of her, but I want you to use her all the same.'

Casey decided to be blunt. 'Are you asking me to use an unknown girl for this assignment?'

'Not *asking*, no.' There was a gentle stress on the word that made Casey's face tighten.

'Just how much experience has this girl had?' she demanded.

'At modelling—none.'

Casey stared at him, allowing her indignation to show now. 'Do you realise what you're saying? I thought you wanted this calendar to be a winner; an amateur could quite easily ruin...'

'But I'm quite sure that with you to tell her what to do she'll be a success,' Ivo interrupted firmly. 'Lucy goes with you, Casey.'

'Or there's no calendar at all, that's what you're saying, isn't it?' she said bitterly.

But Ivo was completely calm as he nodded and said, 'Yes, that's exactly what I'm saying.'

She glared at him for a moment, her mind racing, and then Casey got to her feet and picked up her portfolio. 'In that case I have little choice, haven't I? All right, we'll include your—model in the team.'

Ivo, too, got languidly to his feet, but there was a note of distinct menace in his voice as he said firmly, 'Good. But please don't get any ideas about conveniently forgetting to use her once you get to Lanzarote—because I shall be coming along myself to make sure that you do.'

CHAPTER TWO

WHEN Casey burst into Steve's office an hour later her face was still set in rigid anger. He took one look at her, jumped to his feet, and swiftly grabbed her arm. 'What is it? What's happened? Did Maine turn down your ideas?'

'Turn them down? On the contrary, he thought they were great,' Casey said fiercely, her teeth gritted. 'In fact, he thought they were so good he's going to have a contract drawn up.'

'So why are you so all fired up? I don't see what there is to be mad about.'

'Because there's a condition, that's why!' Casey threw her portfolio on the floor, seething with anger.

'A condition?' Steve stared at her. 'Oh, no, he didn't make a pass at you, did he?'

'At me?' Casey laughed harshly. 'No, it isn't me he's interested in, but you're on the right track.' She paused, trying to control her anger. 'We only get the contract on condition that we use his—his girlfriend, mistress, I don't know what she is—as one of the models!'

'Oh, nice.' Steve let her go of her arm. 'What did you say?'

'What could I say? If we want the contract, we have to go along with him.'

'Who's the model? Is she any good?'

'It's difficult to tell,' Casey said in sarcastic anger, 'on account of the girl never having worked before.'

'Hell!' Steve balled his hand into a fist and brought it down hard on his desk. 'What does he take us for—a modelling school?'

'I just wonder if his bosses know what he's up to. He's using a hell of a lot of the company money just to promote his girlfriend's career.'

'Well, don't get tempted to tell them, or we'll lose the contract altogether,' Steve said practically. 'Maybe it won't be that bad. Perhaps we can just use this girl in the background in a couple of shots; get round it that way. And we can . . .' He stopped as he saw Casey shaking her head. 'No?'

'I've already thought of that, but Maine thought of it even before I did. He informed me that he intends to come with us to Lanzarote. Just to keep an eye on how his company's money is being spent—and to make sure we use his precious girlfriend, of course.'

'I wonder what she looks like,' Steve remarked, momentarily intrigued. 'She must be quite something if she can make a man like Ivo Maine go to these lengths for her. Personally, I wouldn't have said he was the type to make a fool of himself over a woman.'

'There isn't a man alive who hasn't made a fool of himself because of a woman at some time or another,' Casey declared roundly. She glared at Steve as if he were responsible, and he pulled such a comic face that she burst out laughing. 'All right, I'll admit that I'm very glad men occasionally make fools of themselves—but not in this instance.'

Steve immediately sobered. 'No, you're right. And having Maine along is going to be a drag. Do you think you can cope? I can cancel the contract, if you'd rather,' he offered generously.

Casey sighed but didn't hesitate to shake her head, her thick, red-gold hair brushing her shoulders. 'Don't tempt me. But to turn down the contract just because I'm in for a rotten few weeks wouldn't be very professional, now would it? I shall just have to try and make the best of this girl, I suppose. Although I must admit that I'm very prejudiced against her.'

'That's natural enough. But as you say, you'll just have to be as professional about the assignment as possible. Don't forget, you're the expert. And I'm quite sure that both the girl and Ivo Maine will be as anxious as we are to create a really outstanding product.'

Her mouth twisting wryly, Casey said, 'Which means that I've got to somehow turn the girl into a photographic miracle, and Ivo will probably turn round and take all the credit. Whatever happens, I can't win.'

'Yes, you can,' Steve grinned. '*We'll* know it, and we'll get more orders. And isn't that the whole idea?'

'Yes, I suppose so.' Casey turned to go to her own office. 'So now I'd better go and start trying to book a photographer and some models, and try to explain to them that we're bringing along an unknown who expects to be used and treated on a level with girls who have spent years learning their craft.' She paused and then said, 'Is Ivo married, do you know?'

Steve shrugged. 'I've no idea. I haven't heard him mention a wife.'

'Possibly because he's far more interested in this girl, Lucy Grainger,' Casey said acidly. 'I wonder if his wife knows about her, or whether it's all supposed to be a big secret. Well, either way I feel very sorry for his wife; it must be hell to be married to someone who's besotted over another woman.'

It took almost two months of extremely hard work before the photographic team was ready to leave for Lanzarote. During that time Casey had spoken to Ivo on the phone a great many times, but she hadn't seen him. Her first call to him had been a very cool one suggesting that Lucy Grainger take some modelling lessons. 'It would help if your—er—protégée had at least some idea of how to stand and pose,' Casey pointed out.

Ivo's answer was crisp. 'That's already in hand.' And he named a very famous modelling school where Lucy was taking a course.

'I see. I also need to know whether she's a blonde or a brunette, and her measurements for the costume designers. Perhaps you could find out and let me know, or else send along her portfolio.'

'Portfolio?' Ivo queried.

'Oh, sorry, I forgot,' Casey said in mock innocence. 'All professional models have a portfolio of photographs and measurement details available for employers. Usually these are supplied by the agency acting for the model, but as you seem to be acting as the agent for Miss Grainger...'

'A portfolio will be on your desk by tomorrow afternoon,' Ivo said curtly. 'And in the meantime, I can tell you that Lucy is a brunette, she's five foot eight, and her measurements are thirty-two, twenty-two, thirty-four. Is there anything else you require, Casey?'

Managing to hide her catch of breath, Casey said, 'Not at the moment, thank you,' and rang off, feeling rather like a child that had been put firmly in its place.

Again she felt a surge of disappointment, but why she should have she didn't know. It was only to be expected that Ivo would know his mistress's body so well that he could give her measurements off pat like that. And the girl did at least seem to have the figure for a model. Whether she also had the face or not Casey had to wait until the following day to find out when the portfolio was brought round to the office by special messenger, as Ivo had promised.

She did have the face, was perhaps even *too* pretty. Casey took out the first of the photographs and stood looking down at it; Lucy had short, curly, dark hair and a vivacious heart-shaped face. She was also very young, not more than eighteen at the most, Casey guessed. Was that the attraction? she wondered. Was Ivo so jaded that he went for young girls? She felt slightly sick and then was angry with herself, finally admitting that her own initial liking for Ivo was making her feel this way. Because it had been so long since she had been even remotely attracted to anyone, she had expected him to be everything that a woman hoped and looked for in a man, and so it felt almost like rejection when Ivo had turned out to be as fallible as everyone else. Well, the thing to do was to learn from it; wasn't that what Mike had always said? 'Whatever happens to you, no matter how bad, you must always learn from it, learn and grow, so that you'll be better able to face the future.' She could hear his voice now, in the good times and the bad— the terrible times towards the end. Tears pricked her eyes, but she brushed them angrily away; Mike wouldn't think she'd grown much if she succumbed to tears for so little reason, just because a man had turned out to be weak and hypocritical like so many others.

Of necessity, Casey had had to phone Ivo about the assignment a great many more times during the ensuing weeks, but their conversations had been strictly business, and kept short and cool. That the coolness was mostly of her own making, Casey was quite aware, but she didn't see why she should also be hypocritical and pretend to like having an unknown girl thrust upon her. So she had shown her disapproval and Ivo had reacted predictably; he had become equally cool and distant, their former rapport disappearing beneath a façade of businesslike efficiency.

Casey spent many long hours with the costumiers, the photographer, and in their own art studios, getting as much preparatory work done as possible before they left for Lanzarote. She also ran up a large phone bill making calls to the island to arrange for accommodation, transport, an interpreter, and all the other thousand and one details that had to be seen to before the team could actually begin to take the hundreds of photographs from which they would eventually select just twelve for the calendar.

At last, at the end of April, they were ready to go. Casey had sent Ivo the flight tickets for himself and Lucy Grainger, but the two didn't turn up until Casey and the rest of the team had checked in and gone through to the departure lounge. She had half begun to hope that they wouldn't turn up at all, but then Casey saw Ivo come into the lounge and stand by the door, looking round. Her eyes rested on him for a moment, thinking how good he looked in a dark grey suit, but then her gaze shifted to the girl beside him. Lucy had obviously dressed to look the part: she wore very high heels to make herself taller, and a long-skirted linen suit in the latest drab grey colour, together with lots of costume jewellery and a beret anchored to the side of her swept-up, artistically arranged hair. Presumably this was all meant to give her an elegantly casual appearance, but it didn't succeed. She hadn't yet learnt how to carry off that kind of look, how to wear fashionable clothes, however way-out, without worrying about how she looked or what sort of reaction she was getting.

Ivo had noticed Casey now and walked across the lounge towards them, the girl trotting along beside him, her face lit with eagerness. But Lucy's face fell almost ludicrously when she reached them and saw the way they were dressed. The whole team, models included, were old hands at the game and always wore slacks or jeans and sweaters to travel in, putting comfort far ahead of elegance when it came to spending hours on planes and coaches. Of them all, Casey was probably the most sophisticatedly dressed, and even she was wearing a trouser suit. The others turned when Ivo and Lucy came up, and there were quite a few broad grins when they saw her. Casey hadn't said anything, but word had soon got round that they had to work with a complete amateur, and they didn't like it any more than Casey did.

Lucy's face flamed as she saw them grin, and for a moment Casey felt a twinge almost of compassion, but quickly stifled it; even if the girl was young, she must know what she was doing, especially to have twisted Ivo round her little finger in the way she had.

Ivo's face had hardened as he took in the little scene, and he reached down to take hold of Lucy's hand, giving it a comforting squeeze. The gesture gave Casey an absurd stab of jealousy and she said, 'Good morning,' more abruptly than she'd intended.

'Good morning. May I introduce Lucy Grainger,' Ivo answered just as curtly.

Casey nodded to the girl and introduced the rest of the team in turn. There were quite a few of them: there was the photographer, Chas, a man very well-known in his field, and his two assistants; four models—three female and one male; the make-up and costume girls, and a hairdresser. Together with Ivo and Lucy, that made twelve people who Casey had to supervise, take care of, and keep happy for the length of time it would take to do all the shots. Ivo began to chat to the photographer, but in his well-cut suit he looked as out of place among the team as Lucy did. Casey wondered briefly how he had justified his absence from Vulcan to come with them, and also in what role he saw himself other than Lucy's protector. Her protector in every sense of the word, perhaps, on this trip, because Casey was afraid that the other models might not treat her very kindly.

Casey stood with her back to Ivo as she talked to the make-up girl, but she listened to his conversation with half an ear and perhaps more than half her attention, and she heard him determinedly bring Lucy into the conversation, the girl answering with a little giggle of nervousness in every sentence. Their flight was called and Casey threw Lucy a frowning, contemplative glance; she somehow didn't seem the type of girl to become a man's mistress, or to have the cunning to coerce him into getting her this job. Ivo must be in love with her, Casey thought in a flash of intuition; perhaps Lucy only said that she'd like to be a model and he set this up for her off his own bat.

He certainly looked as if he was very fond of her from the way he was smiling at her, and that gesture when he'd taken her hand earlier had been very revealing.

Having arrived after the others, Ivo and Lucy sat together in a different part of the plane, but when they landed in Lanzarote they all boarded the coach that Casey had arranged to have waiting and which she had hired for the whole of their stay. The weather in London had been quite cool when they had left, the skies grey and on the verge of yet another April shower, but in Lanzarote the temperature was at least twenty degrees warmer, only the breeze that swept across the island from the sea keeping it cool.

Once all their equipment had been loaded on the coach, they set off towards the south of the island to the little fishing village of Playa Blanca, where Casey had rented six bungalows in a new holiday development. None of the other members of the team had been to Lanzarote before, and they exclaimed in surprise when they saw how weird the landscape was. But the island was different now than it had been in February; the hibiscus planted in the black volcanic ash at the side of the roads were in full bloom, and every house had at least one brilliantly coloured bougainvillaea climbing up to the roof. Casey looked to see how Ivo was reacting and he seemed as fascinated as everyone else, leaning past Lucy, who sat beside him, to get a better look and point out features that caught his eye.

The sea came into sight and soon the coach pulled up on the road alongside the bungalows. Casey left the photographer to supervise the unloading and went into the reception area to register and collect the keys. She had managed to get only six bungalows, two three-

bedroomed, three two-bedroomed, and one with a
single bedroom that she intended to keep for herself.
Going outside to where the others were waiting, she
gave the three model girls one of the three-bedroomed
bungalows and put the hairdresser, costumier, and
make-up girl in the other. Two of the two-bedroomed
bungalows she gave to the photographer, his two assistants and the male model. They went off, carrying
their luggage, and Casey held out the key of the last
two-bedroomed bungalow to Ivo. 'It's number six,'
she told him. 'Over there to the left past the pool,
according to the plan.'

He took the key and glanced at it. 'And what
number is Lucy in? Is she sharing with you?'

There was an aviary with several canaries flying
around in it over by the pool; Lucy had gone over to
look at it and was out of earshot. Casey gave a short
laugh. 'I hardly think that was the idea, was it? No,
she's sharing with you, of course.'

An angry expression came into Ivo's eyes. 'And just
what makes you presume that I wish to share with
Lucy?'

'Oh, come on! That was one of the main reasons
for setting this whole thing up, wasn't it—so that
you'd have an excuse to come over here and be with
her? Why pretend about it? Surely I'm doing you a
favour by——'

'I don't need favours from you or anyone,' Ivo
snapped. 'Who are you sharing with?'

Casey gave him a wary look, her hand tightening
on the last key. 'I have to have plenty of space to set
out my designs and drawings.'

'In other words you have a bungalow to yourself.
How many bedrooms has it?'

'One, and I'm not sharing it or changing it,' Casey said emphatically.

'May I remind you that *I'm* the one who is paying for this assignment,' Ivo gritted out.

Casey's chin came up defiantly. 'I don't give a damn whether you're paying or not. I am *not* going to share with anyone—and especially not with your dolly-bird!' she exclaimed vehemently.

'Quiet!'

Glancing round, Casey saw that Lucy had come up behind her and had evidently heard her last remark. The girl's face was pale, but whether with anger or not Casey couldn't tell. Casey almost apologised, but then thought, no, why the hell should I? Instead she bent to pick up her cases and walked down the path to her own bungalow, number thirteen.

All the members of the team had been given an outline schedule, but there wasn't enough time left that day to start work. After they had unpacked, most of them drifted over to the bar by the pool to rest and chat. It took Casey rather longer to unpack as she had to set out her typewriter and files, her drawings and art equipment, turning the sitting-room of her bungalow into an office-cum-studio. Afterwards she showered and put on a cool shirtwaister dress, added make-up and brushed her bell of hair until it shone. It was still light when she walked through the complex to join the others, but the sun had begun to set, turning the sky to a glowing pink colour that promised another beautiful day tomorrow. To reach the bar Casey had to pass the bungalow she had allotted to Ivo and Lucy. They came out of the door just as she neared it, and walked through the small flower-filled garden to the path. They had seen her, and it would have been impossible to just hurry past, but Casey's steps slowed anyway. They were, after all, part of the same team, and however much she disapproved of what Ivo was doing it would be much better if there was as little awkwardness as possible.

So she waited for them to reach her, then nodded and said, 'Good evening. I hope you find the bungalow comfortable?'

Lucy seemed reluctant to answer, looking at Ivo who remained silent, and then saying stiltedly, 'Yes, it's fine, thank you.'

They fell into step beside her and walked over to the bar where the others were grouped round a couple of tables outside on the terrace. Casey hesitated, wondering whether she ought to sit with Ivo and Lucy or join the others, as she would rather do. But the decision was taken out of her hands. Ivo picked up one of the metal tables and brought it over, enlarging the group so that they all sat together.

Casey said a general hello and sat down at a chair that Ivo placed for her next to Lucy. He then asked everyone what they would like to drink, and went to the bar with one of the other men to get them. At the tables there was an awkward little silence for a moment until the girls began to talk among themselves again, picking up their conversation where they had left off. Mostly they talked shop, comparing assignments, discussing which were the best agencies, finding acquaintances in common—the usual things. Casey was used to it and could join in, but Lucy sat silently, an onlooker in an alien world, a wistful, unhappy look on her young face.

That the girls were deliberately shutting Lucy out was easy enough for Casey to guess, and she wasn't surprised when Ivo realised it too. He had brought the drinks and sat down on Lucy's other side. She turned to him gratefully, her eyes appealing, and he threw a swift glance round the tables, taking in the situation at once. His mouth hardened a little and, turning to Casey, he said in a louder voice than necessary, 'Have you made any arrangements for going out to dinner?'

She gave him a surprised look. 'Why, no, I . . .'

But before she could go on he gave a challenging look round the group and said, 'Then I suggest that we stick together *as the team we are*, and all go to a restaurant together.'

The others had fallen silent, none of them wishing to take up his challenge, the harshness in his voice having reminded them that Ivo was in a sense paying their wages, and probably had the power to break their contracts if he felt bloody-minded enough.

He was paying Casey's fee too, but she didn't intend to behave like a doormat because of it. 'A nice idea, but not very practical, I'm afraid. The restaurants around here get very crowded, and I'd be very surprised if we found one that could seat us all. And as we haven't booked we'll probably have to go from one restaurant to another as it is. So I really don't see how—— '

She broke off as Ivo got to his feet. 'Excuse me a moment.'

He went off to the bar again and was gone for a little time, but when he came back he stood and looked at them all until he had their undivided attention. 'It's all fixed,' he told them with a grim little smile. 'I've found out the name of a good restaurant close by which has agreed to reserve a table for us tonight . . .'

he paused and looked at each one in turn, finishing at Casey, 'and every night.'

'*Every* night?' It was Chas's, the photographer's, voice that was raised in protest. 'You seem to forget, Ivo, that we're going to be working together every day for what could be a few weeks. Quite frankly I think we're going to occasionally need a break from each other, and I for one don't fancy the idea of trooping around as if we're in a school party all the time.'

There was a general murmur of agreement which didn't seem to perturb Ivo in the least. Turning to Chas he said, 'You are of course free to eat wherever you please—but may I remind you that my company will only be paying for meals eaten at the restaurant where I have booked a table?'

'That's highly unorthodox,' Casey protested.

'I don't see why. If we'd been staying at a hotel, all the meals would have been eaten in the hotel, so for the purposes of this assignment you will regard the restaurant as an extension of this complex.' There was such firmness touched with arrogance in Ivo's voice that all hopes of intimate or chatty little dinner parties faded reluctantly away. And he was right, Casey supposed; if they had been booked into a hotel they would have eaten in the hotel dining-room, but definitely not at one large table, which was what they found awaiting them when they reached the restaurant a little time later.

The restaurant was called Casa Pedro's and was only a short walk through the village from the complex. It was built on the sea-wall and there must have been a beautiful view in daylight; as it was you could see the lights from all the buildings on the other side of the bay reflected in the gently swelling waters.

Casey made the mistake of stopping to glance at the view and was the last to take her seat, finding that the only spare place was at the end of the table next to Ivo. He held the chair for her and she gave a rather mirthless smile and took her seat, moving the chair along a little so that she wasn't quite so close. He had placed Lucy on his other side and opposite them there were the two photographer's assistants, who were deep into a low-toned conversation that had started at the airport and looked as if it could quite easily go on for the whole of the time they were on the island. So they weren't going to be any help; Casey had the choice of talking to Ivo or a silent meal, and wasn't quite sure which would be worse.

The waiter handed her a menu and she gave her attention to it for much longer than it took her to make up her mind what she wanted to eat, and only put it down when Ivo said with heavy sarcasm, 'I had no idea you were such an indecisive person.'

'Foreign menus are always fascinating,' Casey replied calmly, refusing to be drawn. She smiled at the waiter and gave her order.

'Did you say menus or men?' Ivo asked with a sneer in his tone as he watched the waiter smile back before walking away.

A flush of colour came to Casey's cheeks. 'That was extremely rude and uncalled for.'

'Was it? Well, *if* it was, I apologise.' But his voice sounded the opposite to sorry. 'But you can hardly blame me if I look at things through your eyes, now can you?'

Casey turned to face him, close to anger. 'Just what do you mean by that remark?'

He gave her a taunting look. 'If you immediately think the worst of people, you can hardly complain when they think the same about you.'

She studied his face for a moment, seeing the strength and determination there. She wondered why he was doing this; why bother to pretend when it was obvious to all of them that Lucy was his mistress? A spurt of pity for his wife filled her and Casey turned away, not wanting to look at him any more.

'And I wouldn't have thought *that* about you either,' Ivo said angrily.

'What about me?'

'That you're a coward!' he retorted shortly.

She laughed then, a high-pitched sound that drew several eyes, including Lucy's. 'Well, at least you're right about that. I admit it freely; I'm a great coward. Everything frightens me. Even——' She stopped abruptly, aware of Ivo's sudden alertness. 'Even staying on an island that has over three hundred volcanoes. Did you know that? The last eruption was in 1824, of course, but if you go to the Fire Mountains you'll find that you can't even poke your finger into the ground without burning it, the heat comes so close to the surface.'

She was talking too much and too quickly, and Ivo knew it, but her remarks had served their purpose; several of the others had overheard and asked her questions about the island, wanting to know when they could go to the Fire Mountains.

'Sooner than you think,' Casey told them. 'We intend to take most of our photographs there.'

Deliberately she threw a question down the table to Chas, asking him about the difficulties of getting the right lighting for photographs taken in caves and caverns, and he was happy to embark on what turned out to be a short but technical lecture which hardly anyone understood but to which they nearly all listened politely. That Ivo saw through her ploy was quite clear from his sardonically raised eyebrow, but perhaps he was grateful too, because it made things easier for Lucy.

During the rest of the meal he deliberately set out to start a conversation with someone and then draw Lucy into it, making the others talk to her. It worked well enough; they might begrudge the way Lucy had got the job, but there was nothing they could do about it, and it was quite obvious that if they wanted to stay in Ivo's good books they were going to have to accept her. And Lucy was young and didn't try to push herself forward, which helped. But Casey refused to be drawn into his game, her answers so short they bordered on curtness when he tried to bring her into the conversation. She saw the anger in his eyes and knew that she was treading dangerously, but didn't really care. He had signed the contract for her services and had no power to sack her so long as she fulfilled her part of the deal. Although she'd said that she was frightened, she had no real reason to fear Ivo Maine.

When the meal was over the party broke up. It was still quite early, only ten o'clock, so most split up into small groups and wandered along the promenade or through the village. Casey stayed behind to settle the bill and was given a complimentary bottle of wine, which was rather an embarrassment as she'd intended to go for a walk and didn't want to carry it around with her. Deciding to go back to her bungalow and leave it there, she started back for the complex, but saw Ivo and Lucy ahead of her. There was no fear of catching them up because they were walking quite quickly. Casey's mouth twisted grimly; so for all Ivo's anger he was still heading for their bungalow and a long night with Lucy just as fast as he could.

They were gone from view when she reached the bungalows, so Casey quickly deposited her bottle of wine, put a cardigan over her shoulders, and made her way back to the sea-front. She turned left, away from the lighter part of the village where the new developments with their souvenir shops and nightclubs were springing up. The place was pleasant enough now, it still retained some of its intrinsic sleepiness, but she wouldn't like to come here in five years' time when it might well be just another 'Costa Cement'.

At the very end of the promenade, where a great outcrop of rocks barred any further progress, a series of steps led up to the village, and between the flights had been fashioned beds of exotic flowering shrubs, and seats set on terraces shaded by palm trees. Casey climbed to one of these and sat on the stone seat in a corner shaded from the moonlight, looking out across the darkness to where the tiny lights of another island could just be seen on the horizon. It was so peaceful here. She shut her eyes, listening to the sound of the sea, remembering so many happy times, telling herself that she really had so much to be grateful for.

'Are you waiting for a special pick-up, or will anyone do?'

Ivo's sardonic voice brought her eyes quickly open. 'Well, whoever I'm waiting for, it certainly isn't you,' she retorted.

'Now, *that* I can believe.' He came to sit beside her, ignoring her indignant look. 'So who are you waiting for?'

'Why aren't you with your dolly-bird?' she countered. 'She'll be lonely without you.'

'What makes you so sure that's what she is?'

Casey raised her eyebrows. 'Would you have bothered to come here if Lucy hadn't been coming?'

He gave a short laugh. 'Probably not, no.'

'And would you have gone to these lengths to get her on this assignment unless you were—shall we say—fond of her?' She saw him give a rueful grin and shake his head, his features thrown into light by the moon. 'I thought not; there aren't many men who would put their jobs on the line just because they fancy a girl.'

'I didn't say that I fancied her.'

'Oh, for heaven's sake, anyone can see how protective you are towards her. Why go on pretending?' Casey said in sudden impatience. 'Your wife isn't here to see what's going on, and none of the people in the team are likely to blackmail you, if that's what you're afraid of. They're a broad-minded lot; there are no moralists among them.'

'Except you, seemingly,' Ivo observed drily. His remark startled her, but before she could reply he went on mockingly, 'You're so moral, so strait-laced. Or is it all a pretence?' Reaching forward he gripped her wrist suddenly. 'I think it is. You're no innocent. How old are you—twenty-six, twenty-seven? Yes, I'm quite sure you've had plenty of experience of men.'

His fingers closed on the delicate bones of her wrist and he leaned forward menacingly as he spoke. Casey suddenly knew that if she goaded him or got angry he would try to prove his words by kissing her and by trying to make her respond. Taking a deep breath, she said as calmly as she could, 'Please let go of my wrist.' And waited until he reluctantly released his hold and sat back on the seat. 'Thank you. Why did you follow me here?'

He frowned. 'Why? Basically to ask you why you found it necessary to tell the rest of the team about Lucy. You didn't have to turn them against her. It's going to be hard enough for the child without . . .'

'Child?' Casey broke in angrily. 'For heaven's sake, if you think of her as that, what kind of a man does it make you? How old is *she*? Sixteen, seventeen?' She aped his words mockingly, growing angry again despite herself. 'About half your age? Do you really think that bringing her here is doing her any favours? If she wants to be a model, why don't you let her work her way up just like any other girl? Are you so little of a man that you have to do this to try and impress her?'

She stopped as Ivo got to his feet, his face furious, and dragged her up beside him. 'You just went too damn far!' he said fiercely.

His grip tightened on her arms as he pulled her towards him, but Casey put her hands against his chest, holding him off. 'Let go of me or I'll scream my head off,' she warned him.

He glared at her for a moment, more than half inclined to call her bluff, but saw the determination in her green eyes and slowly dropped his hands and stepped back a little. 'I really believe you would.'

'You're darn right I would,' Casey said feelingly. 'And I'd advise you not to touch me again, because I know how to defend myself.'

'Very wise,' Ivo said grimly. 'I imagine you find it an indispensable skill if you go round insulting everyone as you have me.'

'I just can't stand hypocrisy. Did it never occur to you that, by bringing us here so that you could have time with Lucy, you're turning us into hypocrites too? If you want to be unfaithful to your wife, then that's *your* guilt, *your* burden, but you have no right to use us to provide a cover of respectability for you. I——'

But Ivo interrupted her, his tone sneering, 'Your moral sensibility is becoming boring, to say the least. I would remind you that I have it in my power to put a great deal of work in the way of your company if I so choose. Not only from Vulcan Enterprises, but also from other companies that I could recommend you to. But I'm hardly likely to do so if you keep up this attitude, now, am I?'

Casey gave a gasping laugh. 'Are you threatening me—or trying to bribe me?'

'Neither, merely pointing out that I could be of help to you in the future—so long as you help me now.'

'Threatening, then. And do you really think that makes any difference to me? You can go to hell for all I care!' she said scornfully.

'Really? I wonder if your partner would be of the same opinion. Or whether he would approve of all this high-mindedness.' Casey was silent, realising that Steve would certainly have been more conciliatory. 'Exactly,' Ivo said on a satisfied note. 'So if you don't want me to tell your partner that Decart won't be getting any more work from Vulcan Enterprises, and why, then I suggest that you take Lucy under your wing and make sure that the others are friendly towards her and that she enjoys this assignment.'

He didn't add to the threat, he didn't have to. Casey gave him a look that left him in no doubt that she despised him, and said, 'I was right about you the first time I saw you; I thought then that you were a superpig.'

Ivo's face hardened, but he knew that he had won and said smoothly, 'How flattering. But just make sure that you do what I want.' She didn't answer and he gave a short, triumphant laugh, then turned and walked away.

His footsteps resounded hollowly on the stone paving of the promenade. Casey listened as they faded away, and then turned to look again at the sea. But all the peace had gone from the night now, and the place held only the echoes of Ivo's mockery instead of the sweet memories she longed for.

CHAPTER THREE

HAVING to submit to Ivo's coercion didn't put Casey in a very good mood the next morning. She was too annoyed to sleep very well, so got up early and walked down to the supermarket in the village where she bought a large, fresh roll and some butter and marmalade for her breakfast. It was a beautifully fresh morning, with a breeze blowing off the sparkling sea, the waves breaking in a happy song on the narrow stretch of white sand, not more than a couple of hundred yards long, that was the sole reason for the growth of this once remote village. There had been no one around in the complex when Casey walked through it, but there were several early risers in the village, not only the natives of the island, but also a great many more elderly people, who had bought retirement villas out here in this ever temperate climate.

There were even a few hardy people swimming in the sea, which must still be cool from the night air. Lifting her hand to shade her eyes, Casey watched the swimmers, wondering whether to join them or take a dip in the pool at the complex. But then she stiffened as she saw one man begin to wade back to the shore. It was difficult to see his features when his face was in shadow, but he was too tall and his skin too pale for a Spaniard. His shoulders were broad, and there was a contained strength about his body that made Casey recognise Ivo even though she couldn't see his face clearly. Instinctively she moved back into the shop where he couldn't see her, but continued to watch him through the window.

He ran easily up the beach to where he'd left his clothes, his hair clinging to his head and water running down his muscular body. He looked very fit, without even an ounce of fat anywhere, and looking at him one would never guess at the dissolute life he led. As she watched, Casey could almost envy him his apparent ability to walk so arrogantly through life, not caring about anyone else so long as he got what he wanted—or *who* he wanted. But perhaps she wronged him; it seemed that he had gone to quite some lengths to keep his affair with Lucy secret from his wife. Casey wondered cynically whether he was wasting his time; in her experience wives were always aware of their husbands' infidelities almost from the moment they happened. It took a clever man to keep all traces of his unfaithfulness completely secret.

But then, Ivo *was* a clever man, Casey thought; how else could he have got into a position where he could get his company to spend thousands of pounds to promote his mistress's career? Her eyes lingered on him and she felt a sudden strong stirring of desire deep within her, a feeling that hadn't come to her for such a long time that her cheeks flushed with guilt. Leaving the shop, she went quickly on her way, almost running back to her bungalow.

At nine, everyone assembled by the coach, dressed in shorts and shirts and happy to be in the sun. Casey had a clip-board with a long list of equipment that she was ticking off as it was loaded on board, and didn't see Ivo and Lucy walk up to join them.

'Good morning, Casey.'

'Morning.' She turned round abstractedly, but saw the compelling look in Ivo's face, and remembered their conversation the previous night. She shot him a killing glance, but turned to Lucy and managed a rather wooden smile. 'Hello, Lucy. Why don't you sit next to me today and I'll go through the schedule with you?'

Lucy's face immediately became wary. 'Oh, thanks, that would be great,' she said uneasily. But she turned to Ivo, laughed and said pertly, 'You'll just have to look after yourself this morning.'

Putting his hands over his heart, he pretended to groan. 'You're deserting me. I'm devastated.'

They went to get on the coach and Casey turned back to the job in hand, wondering just why she had been appointed as nursemaid to a girl who was probably more experienced than she was.

But either Lucy was a fantastically good actress or this was her first affair, because she certainly didn't seem at all experienced when Casey went to sit next to her and started talking to her. She was reserved at first, which was only natural after she'd heard Casey calling her Ivo's dolly-bird, but the tension gradually eased and she took an eager interest in the schedule.

'Will—will you be photographing me today?' she asked hesitantly.

'I'm really not sure. It's up to Chas what shots we take. We might not take any at all today if he doesn't like the backgrounds I've chosen. It takes quite a long time to set up a shot, you know.'

'Yes, they told me at the modelling school that you have to spend a long time waiting around.'

Casey looked at her curiously. 'Is it your ambition to be a model?'

'Oh, yes!' Lucy answered fervently. 'I've always wanted to make it my career, but my father didn't approve so I didn't have a chance until...' her face shadowed, 'until Ivo—I mean until recently.'

Casey felt a stab of sympathy for the girl, and would have liked to ask a whole lot more questions, but Lucy had turned her face away and was looking out of the window.

Afterwards they talked about modelling again, but Lanzarote was quite a small island and it only took them half an hour or so to reach a gateway with the sign 'Montañas del Fuego' and the symbol of a long-tailed devil holding a four-bladed spear above his head. This was the entrance to the Timanfaya National Park where the mountains were situated. The scenery here was completely barren, without trees or flowers, as if God had created the land and forgotten to clothe it. But to compensate for the harshness of the land-scape the layers of molten lava which had burnt away the earth had settled into strange, writhing shapes of huge waves and miniature craters, of rock so deep-black and a red so bright in the sunlight that the mountains did indeed seem as if they were still on fire.

They all fell into a tacit silence as the coach climbed higher into the mountains, awed by the hidden fer-ocity that lay just beneath the surface and which could wreak such terrible devastation. But there are few natural wonders—or even disasters—in the world that are not put to commercial use, and the coach soon pulled up in a large car park with a restaurant, viewing platforms and the usual souvenir shop. Casey had already obtained permission for them to shoot there, but she went with Antonio, their driver-cum-interpreter, into the office to tell the official in charge that they had arrived.

It took a little time, and when Casey came out she found that most of her team had wandered off to look at the jet of steam that shot out of a small hole in the mountain a few seconds after one of the park-keepers poured a jug of cold water into it. As Casey came up behind them, she heard Lucy laugh in delight as the keeper let her pour the water in, then she jumped back as the steam burst out, and caught Ivo's arm. 'Wait till I tell Mummy that I've been playing with fire!' she exclaimed.

Casey couldn't help it, she gave an involuntary laugh that made both Ivo and Lucy swing round and see her. Lucy realised what she'd said and her face immediately flamed and she turned and walked, then ran, back to the coach. Ivo strode towards Casey and said in a low, grim voice, 'Is this the way you keep your bargain?'

Casey had regretted the laugh from the moment it had come out, but she wasn't about to let Ivo know that. So she shrugged and said, 'Can I help it if she's so sensitive? And I don't remember any bargain; just you issuing a lot of threats.'

'Which still apply,' he pointed out forcefully.

With a sigh, Casey turned and called out, 'Come on, everyone, we have a job to do.' And she turned and walked back ahead of all the others to the coach.

Lucy was sitting in a different seat, with her back resolutely turned to the aisle, but Casey went to sit next to her anyway. 'Lucy, how old are you?' she asked abruptly.

The other girl didn't answer for a moment, but then said, 'Nearly eighteen,' in a muffled voice.

'I guessed as much. Lord, you make me feel like a grandmother. What job have you been doing?'

'I—I haven't been doing any job. I only left school at Christmas.'

'Good grief! What on earth were your parents doing to——' Casey stopped abruptly. 'I'm sorry, that's none of my business, is it? Look,' she touched Lucy's arm, 'I don't know how you got involved with Ivo, but a girl in your situation has got to learn to be thick-skinned. Especially if you want to be a model. You're not always going to find the way made easy for you like this, you know. Eventually you're going to have to try and make it on your own.' Casey hesitated and gave a quick look round to make sure Ivo wasn't in earshot. 'Whatever Ivo may have said to you; you really mustn't depend on him. Men aren't always that reliable. It's much better for a girl if she makes it on her own; that way she's independent and can live her life as she wants to, not be at some man's beck and call.'

She broke off as the coach began to move and gave Lucy a searching look, hoping that at least some of her advice had been taken in. But later, as they got off the coach again, she saw Lucy go up to Ivo, slip her arm in his and give him a great big smile as she clung to him.

They drove the coach as near as they could get to the first site that Casey had chosen—a wild, lunar-like landscape where you could almost see the heat reflected off the black rocks. Carrying her folder of drawings and photographs, Casey walked round the area with Chas as he decided where to set up his camera, although you could hardly call it walking—the ground was so uneven and the rock petrified into such sharp points that moving over it was both difficult and dangerous. He agreed with her on the suitability of the background, but could find no level piece of ground on which to set up his camera, and so detailed his assistants to make a stand for him.

The hot day moved slowly on, the model they wanted to use made-up and waiting, the others sitting around reading in the shade of the coach or sunbathing beside it while they waited for the photographer's equipment to be set up and ready. Only Ivo was at all active. He had opened what looked like a small metal suitcase to reveal a mobile computer, and was working at some report or other. Casey went into the coach to get some sun-tan oil from her bag, noticed what he was doing, and gave a little smile of derision.

Looking up, Ivo saw her expression and his own features hardened. 'And just what do you find so amusing?'

'Just the idea of you carrying a portable office around, I suppose. Do you consider yourself so indispensable that you can't even take a holiday with your mis—without working?' she amended swiftly as she saw his chin come up.

'No one's indispensable,' Ivo said shortly. 'There isn't anyone whose place can't be filled by someone else.'

Casey's face shadowed for a moment. 'In a large concern like Vulcan, perhaps, but in a small business—or in life—there are some people who can never be replaced.'

Ivo's eyes studied her averted face for a moment, but she lowered her head so that the heavy fall of her hair obscured her features. 'You speak as if you have personal experience of that.' His tone was gentler, but there was a touch of curiosity there too.

'Do I?' She turned to look at him and gave a dismissive shake of her head. 'But surely everyone has heard of examples of small businesses folding because a key man has left or—or is unable to carry on. Tell me, does that computer hook up into the telephone system so that you can send your work back direct to Vulcan?'

'It does, yes. Are we changing the subject?'

Casey's eyes went swiftly to his face, taken aback by his acuteness. 'What do you mean?'

'Are you thinking of leaving Decart? Or is it your partner who might leave?'

'Neither. What makes you think that?'

'The feeling in your voice when you spoke about small businesses folding. Do you get on OK with your partner?'

'Very well.' He gave her a quick glance, his left eyebrow rising slightly, and Casey's face tightened. 'Not as well as that! We're just business partners, and that's all.'

This time it was his turn to give her a derisive look. 'My dear Casey, I never thought anything else. You know, you really will have to clean up that rather nasty little mind of yours. It could get you into all sorts of trouble—if it hasn't already.'

Not lowering herself to answer that one, Casey went outside to rub the oil on her arms and legs. She was wearing just shorts and a sun-top, her body still lightly tanned from her previous visit here in February, but she could feel the heat of the sun prickling her skin and knew that she would burn if she wasn't careful. As she rubbed the oil on her legs she felt eyes on her

and glanced up to find that their male model, Ray
Brent, was watching her with a half-admiring, slightly
contemplative look in his eyes. The look surprised her;
with three very beautiful models in the team, she really
hadn't expected to attract that kind of interest from
him, or anyone else for that matter. But maybe he
just naturally looked at all women like that; Casey
had never worked with him before so didn't know
much about him. She was careful not to give him any
encouragement, turning away to speak to someone else
and standing with her back towards him while she
finished oiling herself.

The morning dragged on. Those people who weren't
working went back to the restaurant for a break and
returned with very welcome cold drinks for those who
were. Casey had brought a coolbox which she had
packed full of drinks that morning, but they had soon
gone.

'Perhaps we could rig up some kind of fridge which
would run off the coach battery,' Ivo suggested.
'Would you like me to speak to the driver about it?'

'If you can spare the time from your work,' Casey
answered with mock politeness.

She caught the gleam of cold steel in his eyes as he
said, 'I see that you're determined to pick a fight every
time we speak to each other. Don't you think that's
rather an adolescent attitude?'

Casey's chin came up. 'Possibly—but you're obviously far more used to associating with adolescents
than I am.' And her eyes went deliberately to Lucy
and lingered there.

To her surprise, Ivo grinned. 'You have a very bright
wit—what a pity you put it to such low purpose.'

'I could say something very similar about you,' she rejoined without thinking.

'Could you?' Ivo's eyebrows rose in amusement. 'And what part of me could that be, I wonder?'

A flush of colour came to her cheeks and Casey turned away in relief when one of Chas's assistants came up to tell her they were ready to start at last.

The next hours passed in slow but progressive activity. There were constant adjustments for light, for the model to be reposed, for a wind-break to be set up; all the dozens of little refinements that went to making an arresting photograph. It took the whole day, and they were all aware at the end that they might not even use any of the shots in the finished calendar.

They were all glad to get back to the complex that evening, more tired after waiting around in the sun than if they had been working physically hard all day. Casey showered and changed into a coral sun-dress, then set out the series of Polaroid shots they had taken that day as a preview before Chas had taken the actual photos they might use. It was gratifying to see how well her original ideas and drawings had come out in the hands of a professional like Chas. There was a real feeling of heat there as the model posed against one of the rocks, the flame colours of her costume seeming like a ripple of lava that still flowed from the crater mouth. But this had been one of the easy shots, almost a rehearsal for the rest.

Casey studied them, going over the difficulties they had encountered today, and deciding that it would be better if tomorrow she went with just Chas and his assistants to the next two or three locations to find out in advance what they might need.

She was so engrossed that she forgot the time and was surprised to hear a knock against the glass panel of her front door. Glancing up, she saw Ivo standing outside and went to open it.

'Are you OK? The others are all waiting to go to dinner and we wondered . . .'

'Oh, lord. Sorry, I forgot the time. I'll just get my bag.' She ran into her bedroom, but when she came out found that Ivo was standing in front of the table and looking at the Polaroids himself. 'Well, what do you think?'

He nodded. 'I shall look forward to seeing the finished product.'

'But you'll withhold judgement until then,' Casey remarked drily.

He gave a small smile. 'It's early days, Casey. Let's wait and see how the actual photographs come out.'

'Just in case Chas forgot to put any film in the camera, I suppose.'

'That wasn't quite what I meant.'

'Wasn't it?' Casey had turned to him rather belligerently, and too late found that he was very close. Again that stirring of desire in the pit of her stomach. She smelt the tang of fresh aftershave, was aware of the width of his shoulders, and his sheer masculine strength.

'No, I merely meant that . . .' His voice faded as he glanced up and saw the message in her eyes that she was too slow to hide.

Quickly she turned away. 'I thought you said the others were waiting. I'm hungry myself.' Going to the door, she went through it and waited for him to follow so that she could lock it, glad of the gathering darkness that hid her confusion.

After apologising profusely to the others, Casey led the way down to Pedro's, making sure that she wasn't last this time and could choose where she was going to sit. Smiling at Chas, she said, 'Perhaps we could talk over our schedule during dinner? I thought we might change it a little now that we've seen some of the difficulties.'

Whether he wanted to talk shop or not, Chas had little choice after that, and sat down next to her with Ray Brent coming to take the seat on Casey's other side. Looking down the table, she saw that Ivo and Lucy were in the middle this time, and guessed that he was going to try to make the others talk to Lucy again. He glanced up, his eyes meeting Casey's, and she expected to get another mocking look, but was mildly surprised to see a frown between his brows.

Lucy seemed happier tonight, Casey noticed as the meal progressed. Several times she heard the young girl's laugh rise above the general chatter, and she seemed to be talking quite animatedly with the people around her from what Casey could see. Not that she got much chance to look at the others, because, as soon as she'd finished discussing her idea for the next day with Chas, Ray Brent tried to monopolise her, asking her questions, the answers to most of which Casey was reluctant to give so that she ended up asking him questions instead. This pleased him, of course, but also seemed to give him the impression that she liked him and was interested in him. Casey sighed inwardly and realised that she would have to set him straight at the first suitable opportunity—but it definitely wasn't here, with so many people in earshot.

Casey was the last to leave again, but Ray waited for her. 'We found quite a good bar further down the beach last night,' he told her. 'They have a couple of English entertainers and it stays open till two in the morning. How about going down there and having a drink?'

'Thanks, but I want to try and phone my partner as soon as I get back.'

'OK, so I'll wait for you.'

She shook her head determinedly, 'Sorry, Ray, but I really don't feel like it. Maybe I'll go at the weekend, if the others are going too.'

'I see,' he said stiffly.

Casey smiled at him, recognising the disappointed tone in his voice and wanting to let him down lightly. 'Why don't you ask one of the other girls? They have more time than I do. And maybe they're available.'

'But you're not?'

'Sorry, no.'

'Well, that's straight enough. But it's a pity; most of the girls I meet are models and they don't seem to have much in the way of conversation. They always talk about themselves the whole time. And the photographers are almost as bad; with them it's all lights and camera angles.'

Casey laughed. 'Can't get a good pose in edgeways, huh? Poor Ray.' An imp of mischief prompting her, she said, 'Why don't you talk to Lucy? She isn't a fully fledged model yet, but she's eager to learn; you could tell her all about your experiences.'

'Oh, yes, and what about Ivo? He's her boyfriend, isn't he?'

'He says not,' Casey remarked blandly.

'Really? It's possible, I suppose. I noticed that they've got separate bungalows.'

'Have they? But I put them in the same one.'

'Yes, but I went into reception the first day we arrived, and Ivo was in there asking them to give him a separate one. He's in one over on the other side of the pool now, near you.'

'Is he?' They reached the complex and she handed Ray a bottle of complimentary wine from the restaurant. 'Look, I can see some of the others over by the pool; why don't you take this and share it with them? And I've got one that Pedro gave me yesterday if you'd like to come to my bungalow later to collect it.'

'OK, thanks. But aren't you coming to join us?'

'Depends on how long this phone call takes.'

Unfortunately an elderly resident was already using the phone when Casey went into the reception area. She sat down to wait, but the man had evidently been saving up his phone calls because he made several before at last putting the phone down nearly an hour later. Then, of course, Casey found it difficult to get through and had to keep on trying until she was eventually successful; she gave a sigh of relief as she heard Steve's voice on the other end.

'Hello, Steve, it's Casey. Sorry to call you so late, but I've had a terrible time trying to phone. Is everything running smoothly at the office?'

They talked business for some time before Steve asked how it was going at her end.

'Not too bad; we did one lot of shooting today.'

'What's Ivo's sex-kitten like?'

'Honestly, you men. You have a one-track mind.'

'Cut out the insults and tell me what she's like,' Steve commanded.

'Very young,' Casey said slowly. 'And rather naïve, I think. Pretty, but by no means sensational. The other models here are far better-looking.'

'So what's the attraction? She must have something if he's that crazy about her.'

But Casey was unable to tell him; on the surface Lucy seemed too nice a girl to be any man's mistress, and although she was obviously on familiar terms with Ivo she didn't appear to be in love with him. From what Casey could remember of that period of her own life, Lucy didn't even seem to have a schoolgirl crush on him. But perhaps it was Lucy's innocence that Ivo found so fascinating. The thought made Casey cringe a little, and she quickly changed the subject, asking if there had been any calls for her.

'Only one. Your cousin called and wanted to speak to you urgently.'

Casey groaned. 'Oh, not again. What did she want this time?'

'Usual thing; to cry on your shoulder. Seems she and her husband had another row.'

'I do wish Tina would find someone else to confide in,' Casey sighed. 'I like her husband and I hate being put in the position of having to take sides.'

'Can't say I blame you,' Steve agreed. 'Anyway, she wanted to know when you would be back, and when I said possibly not for some weeks she tried to get your phone number in Lanzarote from me.'

'You didn't give it to her?' Casey said in horror.

'Of course not. But she wasn't very happy about it. I've instructed Heather to tell her I'm out if she calls again.'

Casey laughed. 'Thanks, I appreciate it.'

Putting down the phone, Casey found that Ray and three of the other members of their team were still sitting in a sheltered corner of the patio. She called goodnight to them, but Ray got up and said, 'You mentioned something about another bottle of wine.'

'Of course. Would you like to come with me and get it now?'

'Thanks.'

Ray fell into step beside her and they strolled along through the gardens to her bungalow, the way softly lit by the miniature lampposts that dotted the complex. Casey unlocked the door and turned on the bright porch light before going inside to fetch the bottle which she'd left on the table in the sitting-room. 'Here it is. I——' She broke off as she turned and found that Ray had followed her inside, pushing the door shut behind him.

'Casey,' he said huskily, 'are you sure you're not available?'

'Quite sure,' she answered firmly.

'But you haven't even given me an audition yet. You never know, you might be agreeably surprised.' And Ray drew her to him and put his arms round her. 'Why don't we try it?'

'Ray, will you please . . . ?' But her protests were stifled as Ray covered her mouth with his own and kissed her.

He was big and he was holding her closely, but Casey had little difficulty in making him let her go. She just poked him hard in the side as Mike had taught her.

'Hey, that hurt!'

'It was meant to. I told you I wasn't interested, Ray, and I meant it. Now, will you please take the wine and go? And don't sulk; I can't stand men who sulk. You can't win them all, you know.'

'No, but a man has to try.' He gave her his best crooked grin. 'No hard feelings, huh?'

'Of course not. I'm really quite flattered.'

Ray grinned. 'You're not, but thanks anyway. You're a kind girl, Casey. I envy your man,' he said in a maudlin mood. 'Goodnight.'

'Goodnight.'

Casey thankfully opened the door and half pushed him out into the porch. She had tasted the alcohol on his lips when he'd kissed her, and felt no animosity at all, but she wasn't very pleased when he kissed her again. She drew quickly back and watched as Ray sighed and shrugged, then turned to walk away. But it was only then that Casey became aware of someone on the path that led past the group of bungalows. Lifting her head, she saw that Ivo was standing there, a grim look on his set face, but when he saw that she had noticed him he gave a twisted kind of smile.

'I was going to wish you goodnight,' Ivo said in heavy sarcasm, 'but you would appear to have had one already.'

Ray thought he was talking to him and said, in happy unawareness of Ivo's innuendo, 'Oh, yes, it's been a great evening, thanks.' And went on his way back to the bar.

But Ivo lingered and, when Ray was out of earshot, said scathingly, 'It seems you don't practise what you preach.'

Casey was silent, not seeing why she should go into lengthy explanations that he wouldn't believe anyway. She was painfully aware that he had probably seen the first kiss that Ray had given her as well as the second; the curtains in her bungalow weren't drawn, and the door they had been standing in front of was merely a panel of plain glass that anyone could have seen through.

'I see you're not rushing to defend yourself,' Ivo commented sarcastically.

'No.'

He gave her a puzzled look. 'Is Ray your boyfriend, or whatever euphemism they're using for lover these days?'

'No, I never met him before this assignment.'

'Well, it certainly didn't take you long to get to know him—and get to know him really well, by the look of it,' Ivo snapped on a sharp note of anger. 'But then, moralists always turn out to be the biggest sinners.'

'Maybe you shouldn't judge by appearances,' Casey retorted, stung into anger.

'Why not? Isn't that what you're doing with Lucy and me?'

Casey's eyes widened. 'The situation is hardly the same.'

'How would you know?' Ivo demanded on a low, fierce note. 'Has it ever occurred to you to get your facts right, or even to give us the benefit of the doubt before you go spreading rumour and scandal about us to everyone here? This was going to be a highlight in Lucy's life, but you soured it for her even before she got here. If I hadn't had the foresight to come with her and more or less force people to speak to her, the poor kid would be having a terrible time. And she would probably have been put off modelling for life. And all because you resented having to use her!' he added in disgust.

'Well, if I and the other models resent her, she has you to blame for it,' Casey retorted hotly. 'They've spent long, hard years learning their craft in order to win a place on an assignment as prestigious as this. They're top models and they can pick and choose who they work for, but the fee you're offering and the opportunity of being photographed by Chas created some competition for this shoot. So how do you think they felt when they were told they had to work with a complete amateur or else there was no calendar? And how do you think the other models that I had to turn down felt?' She paused for breath, her chest heaving. 'It's no wonder they're unwilling to accept her.'

Ivo heard her out, but said scathingly, 'You didn't have to tell them.'

'You're right, I didn't have to—because they already knew. One of the models has a friend whose sister works in the model agency where Lucy went for her lessons. It seems that Lucy couldn't resist telling the other girls that she was coming here, and the word soon spread along the grapevine. The modelling world is quite a small and close community, you know.'

'I'm learning,' Ivo said shortly. He looked at her moodily for a moment, his lower lip, the fuller, sexy one, pouting slightly. 'All right, I apologise for accusing you, but it still doesn't alter the fact that you and everyone else have jumped to the conclusion that Lucy and I are having an affair.'

'What else are we expected to think?' Casey demanded exasperatedly. 'If the circumstances are different, why don't you explain?'

'Have you just been to bed with Ray Brent?' Ivo returned shortly.

Casey glared at him, momentarily bewildered by the swift change of subject. 'No, I haven't—not that it's any of your damn business!'

'So why don't you explain what you were doing together?'

'Why the hell should I?'

'Which is exactly how I feel,' Ivo said with some satisfaction. 'Why the hell should *I* explain why I've chosen to help Lucy just because a crowd of petty-minded people have decided to put the worst possible interpretation on it?'

Surprised into silence by his argument, Casey could only stare at him for a moment until she said gropingly, 'If—if we're wrong, then it would be much better for Lucy if you did explain.'

'You *are* wrong,' Ivo said coldly. 'And I have no intention of explaining my actions to you or any of the others.'

'Then you can hardly expect them to give you the benefit of the doubt, can you?' Casey answered just as coolly, stifling her own uncertainty.

'Them—or you?'

'All of us. You had no hesitation in accusing me of—of going to bed with Ray, so why should we think any differently of you?'

'Somehow I still think you're speaking for yourself,' Ivo said disparagingly. 'And as for my accusation—as you've assured me there's nothing between you and Ray, then I withdraw it—and apologise for jumping to conclusions.'

'Even though I haven't explained what he was doing here?'

'No. I'm willing to accept your word.'

'Are you?' Casey looked at him for a moment, then shook her head. 'It's late and I'm tired. I'm going to bed.'

'Ducking the issue, Casey?' Ivo asked sneeringly.

'If you like to look at it like that. If Lucy isn't your girlfriend, then who is she? Or what is she? A financial investment? Are you acting as her manager because you think she has a brilliant career as a model ahead of her?'

He gave a laugh so harsh that Casey's face tightened and she turned to go in, but Ivo reached out and caught her arm. 'One day, perhaps, I might tell you who Lucy is—but not until you apologise for tainting us with your own evil-minded thoughts. And when you apologise you're going to do so to her as well as me, and you're going to mean it. Do I make myself clear?'

She turned to glare up at him. 'Well, maybe I will apologise—if the day ever comes that I don't think that you're lying through your teeth just to cover yourself in case your wife finds out!'

'My wife?' Ivo's mouth twisted into a smile that was so sadistically mocking, it sent a shiver of fear up Casey's spine. 'I'm afraid that's another false conclusion that your warped little mind has jumped to.'

'I don't understand. What do you mean?'

'Why, simply that I have no wife. I'm not married and I never have been. Sorry to disappoint you.' And Ivo gave her a little push as he released her arm, almost as if he felt contaminated by her touch; then he turned on his heel and walked rapidly away.

CHAPTER FOUR

IT WAS the following evening before Casey saw either Lucy or Ivo again. She had hired a car and gone with Chas and his assistants to look at the other backgrounds she had chosen for the shoot. The day had been very hot and rather gruelling, so the first thing she did when they got back to the complex was to put on a swimsuit and dive into the pool. It was an ornamental rather than practical pool, roughly cloverleaf shaped with a small island in the middle. Casey began to swim round it, but bumped into someone and stood up, shaking the water from her face.

'Sorry, I wasn't looking where I was—— Oh, it's you.'

'Hello, Casey. Had a good day?' Ivo answered, his mouth twisting ironically at her change of tone.

'Yes, thanks. Er—did you?' Then, with a frown, 'I thought you always swam in the sea.'

'Did you? Now, how do you know that, I wonder?' Ivo asked, his face changing, becoming amused.

Realising that she'd given herself away, Casey tried to retrieve the situation by saying as offhandedly as she could, 'Oh, I noticed you when I was out shopping yesterday morning.' And then, she added quickly, 'What did you all do today? Did Antonio take you on a tour of the island in the coach, as I suggested?'

'No. We don't all have your energy, so most of the others decided to have a lazy day here.'

'But not you,' Casey said in sudden certainty. 'I suppose you were working again.'

'You make it sound like a crime.' Ivo moved to let a swimmer go past, and his leg brushed hers. He glanced at her, but she looked swiftly away. 'You work hard yourself,' he pointed out. 'I seem to remember your partner telling me that you were dedicated to your job.'

'I like my work,' Casey answered stiffly. 'And I try to take a professional attitude to it, yes.'

'So why is it OK for you to work hard and not for me?' Ivo asked reasonably.

She shook her head, but then said huskily, 'Sometimes people need to work for other reasons than——' She broke off. 'Oh, look, there's Chas about to dive in. I do wish I had a camera with me.'

Ivo followed her glance and laughed. 'Yes, I see what you mean. He looks as if a couple of months at a health farm wouldn't hurt him.' But he only watched until Chas had dived in before turning back to Casey to say, 'What did you mean about there being other reasons for working hard?' But he was too late, Casey had already broken into a fast crawl and was disappearing out of sight behind the island. Ivo looked after her, a small frown between his brows, but made no attempt to follow, instead swimming to the side and heaving himself out of the pool.

They met again as they were walking down to dinner, of course, but Casey made sure she kept away from him. At one point, though, she noticed that Lucy was walking by herself, Ivo having been buttonholed by the make-up girl, so Casey went over and smiled at Lucy. 'Hello. Ivo tells me you've been having a lazy day.'

'Yes, sunbathing mostly.' The younger girl's voice was still slightly withdrawn, although her innate good manners prevented her from being openly hostile.

'You must be careful not to get burnt,' Casey warned. 'It wouldn't do to have patches on your body when you're photographed.'

'*Am* I going to be photographed?' Lucy asked, in a tone that implied she doubted it.

'Oh, yes. In a couple of days, I should think. Chas has said that he will probably want to use you when he does the shoot in the grotto.'

Lucy's face lit with pleasure, and Casey felt a stab almost of jealousy when she remembered what it was to be so young and so easily made happy. 'That's marvellous,' Lucy beamed. 'Can I tell Ivo?'

'Yes, of course.'

She watched as Lucy ran back to Ivo and caught at his sleeve, but then Casey hurried on to catch up the next group of people and walk the rest of the way with them.

During dinner Ray and some of the others decided to go on to the bar they had found, and Casey went along with them. It was a small place, about the same size as the shops that adjoined it in the parade, and their group seemed to fill the place. Casey sat on a stool at the bar between Ray and Chas, feeling relaxed and enjoying listening to Chas's gossip about his society clients. As Ray had promised, there was an English couple who played on guitars and sang, the ballads flowing out to the tables on the pavement where people sat in the warm night, some even dancing in the confined space, the people walking by threading their way between the swaying couples.

But they had only been in the bar about twenty minutes when Lucy and Ivo walked in. Holding Lucy by the arm, Ivo walked straight up to the bar where they were sitting as if he had a perfect right to join them. Which he had, Casey supposed. They moved up to make room for them and Ivo found Lucy a stool but had to stand himself. He bought everyone a drink, overriding some half-hearted protests, and joined in the audience around Chas, listening to what he was saying, although his gaze kept straying.

Casey tried to keep her attention on Chas again, but she found it difficult now, especially when she felt Ivo's eyes on her. The guitar-playing couple took a break, coming to chat to the English customers, and the noise level increased by several decibels. As soon as they had finished their drinks Casey insisted on buying another round, not wanting to appear mean, but the place was getting so noisy now that she didn't really want to stay any longer. Chas was having to raise his voice to make himself heard and was looking rather red in the face. Casey looked at him worriedly; he didn't seem to be a terribly healthy person—his waistline was undoubtedly large and he drank too much, although it didn't show in his manner. She devoutly hoped that he wasn't going to be ill; it was so easy to drink more than you realised in this heat.

Her thoughts must have shown in her face, because Ivo moved round to stand beside her and said softly, 'Afraid of having your photographer collapse on you?'

She gave him a rueful look. 'Do you always read minds?'

'Your thoughts were rather obvious.' He glanced at Chas. 'Does he always live at this level?'

'I believe so, but I've only been on short shoots in England with him before. I just pray that he doesn't have a heart attack or something while we're here.'

'No, that would make it rather awkward to finish the calendar, wouldn't it?' Ivo said sarcastically.

'I didn't mean it from that point of view!' Casey exclaimed in protest. 'How can you think that?'

'Why not?' He paused, giving her an ironic look. 'But then, we've already discovered how easy it is to jump to false conclusions, haven't we?' He watched for her reaction, but she turned away until he said, 'By the way, I wanted to thank you.'

'For what?' she asked suspiciously.

'For giving Lucy some encouragement.'

'Why thank me? I was only carrying out your orders.'

'Ah, yes, so you were,' Ivo agreed, but there was no coldness in his voice.

The musicians began to play again and quite a few couples went outside to dance on the pavement, some even spreading on to the strip of ground beyond that ran down to the beach.

'Would you like to dance?' Ivo asked.

She stared at him, wide-eyed, unable to hide her surprise. 'With you?'

'What a reaction! Of course with me, woman!'

'But—but what about Lucy?'

Ivo glanced across to where Lucy was in animated conversation with Ray and one of the models. 'She seems happy enough. Well?'

Casey shook her head. 'No—no, thanks. I . . .'

'Coward,' Ivo said softly, leaning closer and looking into her eyes.

She gazed at him, her face suddenly vulnerable, but made no protest when he took her hand and led her outside.

It was a very gay, continental scene: the warm, starlit night, the tables with their fringed parasols, the people in laughing, holiday mood, drinking and dancing. Ivo put his arm around her waist, drawing Casey close against him, taking her other hand in his firm grip and beginning to move in time to the music. His body and his hand felt hot against hers, but even so Casey shivered, the tremor running through her so that he felt it.

'Relax,' Ivo said softly.

He tried to pull her a little nearer, but she resisted him, her emotions in a crazy turmoil. She didn't know what she was doing here in his arms like this. She didn't even like him, even though he could arouse this feeling of awareness that made her legs feel weak as she tried to dance. There were more people dancing now and there was little space. Lifting her hand, Ivo placed it on his shoulder and put both his hands on her waist. She lifted her eyes to look into his for a long moment, then let him draw her nearer until she was leaning against him, although her heart was beating very fast and she was intensely aware of his closeness.

Casey was quite tall, but her forehead was only level with Ivo's chin, his shoulder just the right height to lean against if she had allowed herself to relax that much. But, even though she was held so close to him, her body was still stiff, her pulses racing.

Ivo's mouth brushed her hair as he looked down to say, 'Why so tense?'

'I—I'm not. Not at all.'

She tried to smile and went to move away from him in some relief when the music stopped, but the musicians almost immediately began to play again and Ivo pulled her back into his arms. They danced on, her nostrils full of the masculine scents of him, the tingling cleanness underlaid with the basic muskiness of his warm skin. She felt his body close against her chest and her hips, his hands firm round her waist, and desire rose like a tide. Casey tried desperately to stifle it, telling herself that it was the heat, tiredness, anything but what it was. But another tremor ran through her and Ivo bent his head and gently touched her temple with his lips.

Immediately she pulled away from him and stopped dancing. 'I'm thirsty. It's really much too hot to dance.' And she turned and went back into the bar.

Ivo followed her more slowly, but Casey was careful to avoid his eyes as she sat at the bar again, and was helped by Lucy catching Ivo's attention as she made some remark to him. Quickly Casey swallowed down her now warm drink, murmured goodnight to those nearest to her and left the bar as unobtrusively as she could, but when she reached the door she glanced back and saw that Ivo was watching her. For a fleeting moment their gaze locked, but Casey dragged her eyes away and almost ran out of the lights into the welcoming darkness.

At first she turned her steps in the direction of the complex, but was afraid of running into one of the team there and having to stop and try and pretend that everything was normal, so instead Casey hurried along the promenade until she came to the stone steps and the seat where she had sat on their first evening. She stayed there for a long time, trying to analyse her feelings and failing completely. It was just sex, she told herself, the frustration of her love-starved body reacting to the heat and Ivo's closeness. She should never have danced with him. But she had danced with other men since Mike had died, some as good-looking as Ivo, and she had never felt even a tingle of desire. Hadn't wanted to—and still didn't. But maybe her body had other ideas than her mind.

Casey leaned against the wall, her chin on her bent arms, and realised that argument wouldn't hold. If it was her body that was so frustrated, why hadn't it reacted like this when Ray had kissed her? And he had kissed her properly, not just brushed her temple with his lips as Ivo had done. And yet here she was, her stomach churning, her heart banging like a drum, and her body shaking. So it had to be Ivo who was the catalyst—and only him. She felt frightened suddenly, and terribly afraid of where these emotions might lead. But that was silly; they wouldn't lead anywhere so long as she was strong. If she just denied them, then they would have to go away and she could go back to the tenuous peace that she had tried so desperately hard to attain.

A shiver ran through her, and Casey realised that the night had turned cold and it must be very late. She began to walk swiftly back to the complex, wishing that she hadn't left it so long. There were very few lights in the houses now, and what street-lights there were had long since gone out. She almost tripped on a piece of broken paving, and the strap of her sandal slipped off her heel. While she bent to pull it back on, she thought she heard the sound of soft footsteps behind her. Quickly she swung round to look. She saw no one, but grew suddenly afraid of the darkness and began to hurry on to the bungalows, her heart beating anxiously until she was safely back.

Some nine kilometres from Playa Blanca the highway was crossed by a minor road that skirted the salt flats and hugged the coastline above cliffs where great rollers broke, sending foam and spray bursting high into the air. The road ended at El Golfo, a bay with a cliff distorted into the shape of a gigantic, petrified tidal wave which was once the inner rim of a volcanic cone. And at the foot of the cliff there was an emerald-green lagoon where the water was always as tranquil as an inland lake, even though the roaring Atlantic was only a few yards away. It was here that the team came the next morning, arriving early, before the place filled with passing tourists.

The coach had to be left in the car park just before the bay and the equipment carried down to the lagoon, which was no real hardship except for the wind. As soon as they skirted the cliffs guarding the bay, a fierce wind, as strong as a sea-storm, caught at them and they had to fight their way down the last half-mile to the sheltered lagoon. There was a path, but the waves beat against the rocks with such violence that they were covered in sea-spray near the top, and farther down they were blasted with particles of sand that stung like insect bites.

They were using Ray and two of the model girls today. They were made ready in the coach, but then had to be covered in blankets to protect them from the wind as they went down to the lagoon. Casey must have gone up and down the path a dozen times in the course of the day, carrying equipment, seeing if the models were ready, asking people to move out of the line of the shot, bringing food and drink. The others helped, of course—Ivo, too—but it was her responsibility and Casey did her work conscientiously. She was glad when Chas pronounced himself satisfied at last and they could load the equipment back into the coach.

It happened that she and Ivo were the last to leave the lagoon, carrying the long, rolled-up wind-shield between them because the wind pushed you off balance if you tried to carry it alone. They had got half-way along the path when a particularly fierce gust lifted the sand and sent a shower of it over them. Casey gave an exclamation and came to a stop, lifting her free hand to her face. 'Oh, this wind!'

'Are you all right?'

Casey shook her head violently, her hair full of sand. 'No, darn it, some sand has gone in my eye.'

'Here, let me take a look.' Putting down the wind-shield, Ivo came and stood with his back to the wind and the sea, sheltering her as she obediently turned to face him. 'Got a handkerchief?'

She gave him one from her pocket and Ivo put his hand on her head, holding it still, as he gently removed the sand from her eye. 'That seems to have got it; how does it feel?'

Casey blinked a couple of times, then said, 'Fine. Thanks.'

She went to move away, but Ivo kept his hand on her head, his eyes studying her face. 'Why did you run away again last night?'

'Run away?' She gave an uneasy laugh. 'Of course I didn't run away. I was tired, that's all. I went back to the complex.'

'Now why, I wonder, do you find it necessary to lie to me?' Lifting his free hand he ran his thumb gently along her jaw line and felt her quiver and flinch away from his touch. 'I saw you come back, Casey—at almost two in the morning, but it was only about midnight when you left the bar.'

'Please let go of me,' she said tensely.

'Certainly—when you've answered my question.'

'Oh, really, this is ridiculous.' She tried to brush his hand away, but he only tightened his hold.

'Is it? Perhaps. But twice now you've run from me like a startled rabbit, and it intrigues me to know why.'

'Possibly because you're very pushy,' Casey answered crossly. 'And also very nosy. What were you doing last night—spying on me?'

'Women always try to change the subject when they have something to hide,' Ivo observed.

'You seem to know a lot about women.'

He smiled a little. 'Enough at any rate to know whether they're—shall we say, interested in me.'

'Well, I'm not, if that's what you're getting at,' Casey said swiftly.

'Aren't you? Perhaps I used the wrong word, then. Perhaps I should have said immune. Because you're certainly not immune to me, are you, Casey?'

She licked lips which were suddenly dry and dropped her eyes, but he still had his hand on her chin and lifted it so that she had to look at him, her eyes angry, almost resentful. Another violent gust of wind sent bullets of sand flying through the air, and they both automatically ducked their heads, their shoulders hunched. Ivo lifted his arm protectively and held her close against him until the gust was past, then said softly into her ear, 'You can't hide from your own feelings, Casey; no one can.'

But she twisted out of his hold and bent to pick up the wind-shield. 'Are you going to help me with this or not? I want to get out of this wind.'

He left it at that and Casey took care to keep well away from Ivo for the rest of the day, and the next morning she said very pointedly that she wouldn't be needing Lucy that day, so why didn't she take the opportunity to go for a ride on one of the camels they'd seen at the Fire Mountains? Lucy had been saying how much she longed for a ride ever since she'd found out that the camel-trains took tourists up the mountain, so Ivo had little choice but to agree when Lucy turned an eager face towards him, but he threw Casey a sardonic look that left her in little doubt of his feelings.

That evening Casey pleaded a headache and didn't go down to Pedro's with the others, although when they were safely out of the way she went over to reception and put through a call to Steve. He told her that her cousin, Tina, had rung again and wanted Casey to phone her urgently, but apart from that everything was going fine. Casey sighed, not wanting to get involved with her cousin's problems, and cravenly decided to put off the call until tomorrow. Going back to her bungalow, she made herself a snack and then sat down to go through the day's Polaroids. The shooting was going well; Chas had sent one of his assistants to the airport with all the film they had shot so far, so that it could be developed in his own studios in London. They expected copies to be sent out to them the next night so that they could make sure the work they had already done was up to the standard they wanted. Nobody wanted to get home to England and then find out that they had to come back to Lanzarote because one set of prints wasn't good enough, or there had been a dud film or something. Stranger things had happened, and always worked out to be extremely expensive.

An idea occurred to her for the next day's shoot in the grotto, and she pulled the paste-ups she had done previously towards her, adding to them while the idea was fresh in her mind. An hour or so later, a knock sounded on the wooden frame of her door. Casey had drawn the curtains tonight and was reluctant to answer, but thought that there might have been some problem over the restaurant bill, so when the knock came again she went to open the door.

She pulled back the curtain, saw Ivo outside, and visibly hesitated, their eyes meeting through the glass. Slowly her hand went to the key and turned it, then she opened the door but stood in the doorway. 'What is it?'

'How's the headache?'

Her face hardened, expecting some sarcasm. 'Terrible. Why?'

'Because in that case I'm sorry to have to disturb you. But Lucy isn't feeling well and I understand that you have all the medication here.'

Casey immediately felt like a heel. Turning back into the bungalow, she picked up the first-aid box she habitually took on assignments with her and rejoined him in the porch. 'What's the matter with her?'

'I'm afraid she might have sunstroke.'

And he was proved to be right, as Casey realised as soon as she saw Lucy. The girl was lying on her bed, but was dressed and was giving little moans of distress, her skin burning hot.

'Hello, Lucy. What have you been up to?' Casey put a hand on her forehead and found it wet with sweat.

'I feel so ill,' Lucy moaned. 'I think I'm going to die.'

'You can't die,' Casey told her practically. 'You're under contract. And besides, you have your first session as a model tomorrow, remember?'

This brought a hiccuping laugh from Lucy, but then she put a hand up to her mouth, her eyes rounding in panic. Casey grabbed her and rushed her into the bathroom where Lucy was horribly ill and then burst into tears.

'Anything I can do?' Ivo put his head round the door.

'Yes, go and make her an ice-pack with the cubes from the fridge.' Gently Casey washed Lucy's face and led her back into the bedroom. 'Come on,' she coaxed, 'put your night dress on and get into bed. You'll start to feel better now.'

'I don't, I feel terrible.'

But Lucy did as she was told, and when Ivo knocked and came in she was lying in bed with a sheet over her, looking very sorry for herself. He had wrapped the ice in a soft towel and Casey took it from him and put it on Lucy's forehead. The girl gave a groan almost of pleasure and closed her eyes in relief. Casey looked at her for a moment and then turned to Ivo. 'What on earth happened to her?' she demanded.

Ivo opened his hands expressively. 'She was fine until we started walking back from Pedro's. She'd been sitting with the costumier and the make-up girl during the meal and was walking with them when suddenly she seemed to collapse, so I picked her up and carried her here.'

'Did you go on the camel-ride this morning?'

'Yes, but she was fine then.'

'Did she wear a hat?'

'No, I suggested she did, but she said she wanted to get her face brown.'

'And you let her get away with it, I suppose,' Casey remarked drily. 'How about this afternoon; what **did** you do?'

'We drove around the island in the mini-moke I'd hired, and then came back here to swim and sunbathe.' He held up a hand as Casey was about to speak. 'But I made sure she didn't lie out there long enough to get burnt.'

Casey frowned. 'Even so, she's had a great deal of sun, but it shouldn't have made her this bad.' She saw that Lucy had begun to shiver so took the ice-pack away and took the girl in her arms as she began to cry, gently rocking her. A thought occurred to her and she said, 'What did she have to drink at dinner? Did you notice?'

Ivo shook his head. 'I was sitting right at the other end of the table with Ray and the other girls and they seemed to be asking me all sorts of questions all through the meal so that I——' He stopped abruptly and looked at Casey. 'I see. You think they did it deliberately,' he said, lowering his voice so that Lucy couldn't hear.

Casey gave an exasperated sigh and nodded. 'I think they might have thought it would be a good joke to get her drunk, yes, especially as she's down to model tomorrow. For her to be this bad they probably laced a couple of her drinks, but they could hardly have foreseen that she would be as ill as this.'

'Damn them!' Ivo said feelingly. 'Don't they care what happens to the poor kid? She was so looking forward to tomorrow.'

Lucy opened her eyes, although they hardly focused properly. 'I'm—I'm going to be sick again.'

After this trip to the bathroom, Lucy was so weak that it took both of them to help her back to the bedroom this time. Afterwards Lucy lay back on the pillow, her eyes closing in dizzy exhaustion.

'I think she'll sleep it off now,' Casey said, looking down at her. 'But I think I'd better stay here with her tonight.' She hesitated and said rather stiffly, 'Unless you'd prefer to stay with her yourself, of course.'

'By no means. You're doing a grand job,' Ivo answered heartily.

Casey gave him an expressive look. 'And you'd rather not have to deal with her if she feels ill again. Men!'

Ivo grinned. 'She'd much rather have you with her than me. And look how efficiently you've nursed her,' he cajoled. 'Anyone would think you'd had experience as a nurse.' He said it as a light-hearted compliment, and was taken aback by the way Casey's face suddenly set into a rigid mask.

Turning away, she said stiffly, 'I'll go over to my bungalow and get my things.'

But Lucy stirred and clung to her hand. 'Don't leave me. Please don't leave me.'

Casey looked down at her rather helplessly, but Ivo said, 'I'll go over and get them, if you like.'

'All right,' Casey agreed reluctantly. 'Here's my key. Just a toothbrush will do.'

Ivo went away and came back about ten minutes later, but he'd brought not only her toothbrush and washing things, but also her nightdress, make-up box, and the novel she'd been reading. Casey's eyes went over the things and her thoughts must have shown in her face, because Ivo said mildly, 'It was merely common sense. Wouldn't you have been able to do the same for me?'

She smiled a little and said, 'Yes, I suppose I would. Thanks.'

'How is she?'

'Out like a light. I don't think she'll be ill again, but she's going to feel terrible in the morning.' And Casey gently stroked the damp hair from Lucy's cheek.

Ivo watched her for a moment, a contemplative look in his grey eyes, but when Casey turned to him he said quickly, 'And she's going to be terribly unhappy about losing her chance to model.'

Casey's face tightened. 'Don't worry; she won't lose her chance. I'll reschedule the shoot so that we do the grotto shots later. *And* I'll have something to say to the others about this.'

'Really? I'd have thought you would welcome the opportunity not to use Lucy. After all, you didn't want her on this shoot, did you?'

'Whether I wanted her or not has nothing to do with it,' Casey answered crisply. 'Or with the others. She's here to work and they deliberately set out to make her ill. It was totally irresponsible and cruel, and I'm going to make darn sure they know exactly how I feel about it.' She paused, her eyes flashing angry fire, and saw that Ivo was looking at her with an arrested expression on his face. 'Well?' she demanded belligerently. 'I suppose you don't believe I'll do it?'

'On the contrary, if I were them I'd be shaking in my shoes.'

The thought of him being afraid of her rather amused Casey and she smiled.

'Don't you believe me?'

'No.' She shook her head and tilted it a little on one side to look at him. 'I don't think there's very much that you're afraid of. You seem so very strong and self-confident.' She paused, colouring a little as she realised how personal she was being.

'Thank you. But you're strong in many ways too. In fact, you seem to have only one weakness.'

Knowing full well to what weakness he referred, Casey hurriedly said, 'I think I'll turn in now; if you remember, we planned to make an early start tomorrow.' And she walked through into the sitting-room and across to the door which she opened for him.

Apparently in no hurry, Ivo strolled after her, his hands in his pockets, and stood beside her. 'You know,' he said, leaning against the doorpost, 'there's a theory that the best way to conquer a weakness is to face up to it. That fear fades before familiarity.'

'But maybe I don't want to be familiar with this particular weakness,' Casey pointed out coolly.

His mouth twisted with amusement, but then his eyes darkened a little and Ivo leaned towards her as if he was going to kiss her. Casey instinctively recoiled, jerking her head back, but Ivo came on, only at the last minute turning his head to gently touch her cheek. 'Thank you for taking care of Lucy,' he said lightly, his eyes alight with mockery and mischief. 'I greatly appreciate it.'

She gave him an enigmatic look. 'Especially as you didn't look after her very well yourself. After all, she is supposed to be under your—protection, isn't she?'

His brows flickered, but Ivo merely said, 'Do you really still think that?'

'You haven't offered any other explanation yet,' she reminded him.

'And I don't intend to. You know that.' He looked into her face intently, holding her gaze. 'Must you judge by presumption? By expecting the worst of people? Why won't you follow your own feelings, Casey, your own heart? Because I'm sure that in your heart you can see how innocent Lucy is. And perhaps, if you'd let yourself, you'd feel differently about me, too.'

She dragged her eyes away, the heart he had spoken of so easily thumping in her chest, but a great feeling of fear and antagonism filling her so that she lifted her head challengingly and retorted, 'Oh, I'm willing to agree that Lucy may still be innocent—but she isn't likely to stay that way for long with you around her, now, is she?'

The words had been deliberately rude; Ivo straightened up, gave her a baleful look, then turned and strode away.

Lucy didn't stir again that night, and when morning came was still in such a deep sleep that Casey didn't attempt to wake her. It was still early, only seven-thirty, when Casey dressed and went over to the bungalow that Ivo had hired for himself. She knocked, but had to knock again before Ivo came to the door, a towel wrapped round his waist.

'Sorry, I was in the shower. Is Lucy OK?'

'I think so; but she's still out. Would you take over from me now and stay with her for the rest of the day?'

'Of course. I'll be there in five minutes.'

He was there almost sooner than that, dressed in a pair of shorts and a sweater, his hair still wet. Casey didn't attempt to talk to him, merely gathering up her things and leaving him to it.

Going over to her own bungalow, she changed and made some breakfast, then walked over to where the rest of the team was gathered about the coach, waiting to go. Glancing over them, Casey saw that everyone was watching her expectantly, most of them with covert grins on their faces. A cold anger filled her, and she made quite sure during the next five minutes that they all knew about it. She told them what they had done to Lucy had been both unprofessional and dangerous, and that if they tried anything like it again she would make darn sure that they would never work for her again and that their respective agents knew why. At first they were inclined to take it lightly, protesting that it had only been a joke, but Casey's scathing contempt got through to them so that several of them had hang-dog looks by the time she'd finished.

'And you needn't think that we're going to go ahead on the grotto shots without Lucy,' she added. 'We'll have to wait until she's well again before we do those. Instead we'll do the reserve shoot at that hole in the cliffs where the sea comes bursting through. I'm afraid it will mean that you'll be out of the sun, that you'll get very wet, and that the models' hair and make-up will have to be continually redone.' She gave them a mirthless smile. 'So maybe by the end of the day you'll be envying Lucy her day in bed. Let's go, shall we?'

That day she worked them all very hard, making doubly sure that everything was perfect, which was rather hard on Chas, who was above playing malicious jokes on people, but made the rest of them realise that life would be a whole lot easier if it didn't happen again.

Everyone was extremely subdued when they returned to Playa Blanca that evening. Instead of giving a hand to unload, as she normally did, Casey left Chas to supervise and went across to Lucy's bungalow. The doors stood wide open to the late afternoon sunlight, so Casey kocked on the glass and Lucy herself came to the door, looking rather pale but apart from that perfectly OK. 'Hello. How are you feeling?'

'Tons better, thanks.' Lucy stood back to let Casey in. 'Ivo tells me that you looked after me and stayed all night.'

'Don't you remember?'

'Not a lot,' Lucy confessed. 'I'm sorry to have caused you so much trouble; Ivo said it was a combination of too much sun and the wine at dinner last night.'

So Ivo hadn't told her it had been deliberate. Casey inwardly congratulated him on his wisdom; it would only be worse for Lucy if she knew they had played such a cruel joke on her.

'How—how did the shoot go?' Lucy asked wretchedly. 'I suppose it was all right because you didn't really want me in it anyway.'

'Didn't Ivo tell you? I put off the grotto shoot until another day. We did a reserve shoot today, and you certainly didn't miss anything—the others hated it.'

'Really?' Lucy looked at her uncertainly. 'Casey, I—I wanted to thank you for looking after me.'

Casey smiled at her. 'I thought you said you couldn't remember. I suppose Ivo told you to thank me. You really don't have to, you know. You're as much part of this team now as any of the others, and it's my job to look after all of you.'

'But you don't like me. You think that Ivo and I...' A big blush spread across her pale cheeks.

Suddenly making up her mind about Lucy, Casey said, 'And I was obviously very wrong and must apologise to you for that. But it did look ...' She gave a dismissive wave of her hand. 'I dare say there could be another reason for such favouritism. Ivo isn't a relation of yours, is he, by any chance?'

Lucy shook her head. 'No, not a relation, but he's—sort of looking after me.'

After hesitating a moment, Casey said, 'Lucy, you'll probably hate me for it, but can I offer you a bit of advice? Whatever you think now, however marvellous you think it is to be on this shoot, Ivo isn't doing you any favours by bringing you here. You see, it won't do your career any good when people know how you got the job. They'll feel antagonistic towards you and it will be doubly hard to get an agent to represent you and for him to get you any more work.'

She had sat down on the settee and now Lucy came to sit beside her. 'I'm beginning to remember things from last night now. You cleaned me up and held me, didn't you?' Casey nodded, and after a few moments Lucy said unhappily, 'If I look all right in these shots, I don't see why other magazines won't give me work. They might. Ivo said all I needed was a start.'

'Oh, Lucy, he knows nothing about this business. How could he? And anyway, he probably only said it to please you. He knew how much you wanted to be a model and probably thought that this would make you gra——' She broke off, deciding to leave Lucy with some illusions left. 'I warned you before not to rely on men,' she reminded the younger girl.

'But I know Ivo will never let me down; he promised to look after me, you see.'

'Lucy, you're so naïve. You can't trust men like that.'

'Why not? Haven't you ever trusted a man?'

Casey was silent, completely thrown by that simple question, and in the hiatus Ivo walked into the room. 'Well?' he asked, his eyebrows raised. 'Isn't there a man you trust? The one whose photo you keep beside your bed, for instance?'

CHAPTER FIVE

CASEY stared up at Ivo, taken aback by his question, then got angrily to her feet. 'How the hell did you know...?' she began heatedly and then stopped. 'Oh, when you collected my things last night.'

'Exactly. But you haven't answered Lucy's question.'

'What?' Casey lifted her head and met Ivo's steady gaze, and knew that he wouldn't let her go or give her any peace until she answered him. She felt hunted, as if she'd been caught in a trap, and hated him for probing into her private life like this. Her heart fluttered and she looked wildly at the door, but Ivo's big frame completely blocked it.

'Well?' he insisted implacably.

Casey looked down at her hands as she twisted them together. Slowly she said, 'Yes, I trusted a man once.'

'Did he let you down?' It was Lucy who spoke, but Casey looked at her almost unseeingly, as if she'd forgotten the other girl was there.

She bit her lip, but then lifted her hands to cover her mouth, as if she was afraid of revealing even that much emotion. Then she gave a harsh, unnatural laugh, 'Yes, I suppose you could say he let me down.' For a moment she swayed on the verge of hysteria. 'It—it's none of your business,' she stammered, and went to plunge past Ivo to the door, but he reached out and caught her wrists, swinging her round to face him.

'But I think it is. You want explanations from me, Casey, but how about some from you? Just what kind of a man is he to make you so bitter—and yet you keep his picture by your bed?'

'What kind of a man?' In a sudden rage, she looked at Ivo venomously. 'He was worth ten of you!'

'Was?'

'Yes, was, damn you!' And, wrenching herself free from his hold, she rushed out of the bungalow.

Casey called on Lucy again the next morning, but thought that she still looked too peaky to work so took the team to another location without her or Ivo. But here they ran into one of the big problems that frequently bedevilled a shoot—spectators. Word had evidently got around that they were on the island, and before very long a small crowd had gathered to watch. It wasn't too difficult to keep the nearer ones out of camera shot, but the particular shot they wanted had a view of the hills in the background, and people would keep walking into the field of vision. Time and again Chas's assistants would try to clear them away, only to have someone else stroll into sight. In the end Chas threw one of his creative tantrums and refused to carry on. 'You'll have to find somewhere else,' he raged. 'I can't possibly work in these circumstances.'

Casey sighed and told them to pack up; it was hot and they were all fed up, so there was no point in trying to force them to work. When they got back to the complex they found Ivo and Lucy stretched out on sun-loungers by the pool. Ivo got up and walked over to Casey, his eyebrows raised. 'You're back early. How did it go?'

'Don't ask,' she replied wearily.

'You look as if you need a drink. Come on.' He led the way over to the bar and pulled out a chair for her at a table in the shade. Casey sat down and leaned back in the chair, closing her eyes with a sigh.

Ivo stood looking down at her for a moment, and then went over to the bar to buy two large, cold gin and tonics. 'I take it you haven't had a very successful day,' he commented as he brought them back to the table and sat down beside her.

'And some.' Picking up her glass, Casey said, 'Cheers,' and took a long swallow, the tartness of the drink like nectar to her parched throat. 'I needed that,' she murmured. She turned, languidly, to look at Ivo. The two days he'd spent here with Lucy, lying in the sun, had tanned his skin to a deep golden tone. He must have rubbed in some oil, because his body glistened in the sunlight, and to Casey's fanciful eyes he looked like a statue, a beautiful bronzed figure that had come to life. She licked lips that had suddenly gone dry again, and remembered that the last time she had seen him they had quarrelled. But then, they seldom met without finishing up having some kind of fight, she realised unhappily.

'You know something,' Ivo said, his eyes intent, 'when you're relaxed you have the most expressive face of any woman I've ever met. You can see all the different emotions chasing each other through your mind. But then you suddenly become withdrawn, as if you had snapped shut a book, and there's only the closed, blank covers to look at.' He paused, leaning closer, and said softly, 'Like now.'

His gaze held hers for a long moment, but then Casey dragged her eyes away. As if he had never spoken of anything else, she said coolly, 'I'm sorry the shoot didn't go well today; there were too many spectators.'

'Are you going to abandon that location, then?' he asked, accepting her change of subject.

'I don't want to; it's perfect for our purposes, but it's difficult to know how to keep people out of the long shots.' Lifting her hand, she fluffed her hair off her forehead then let it fall again. 'But I'll think of something,' she added determinedly.

Ivo grinned. 'I'm sure you will.'

His grin was infectious; Casey's mouth began to twist into a smile before she remembered that she was mad with him. 'How's Lucy?' she asked, looking across at the younger girl.

'Fine now. She'll be able to work tomorrow.'

Casey shook her head. 'No, tomorrow's Sunday. Which is good because it will give everyone time to relax and get over today. Then we can start fresh again on Monday and do the grotto shots.'

'What about spectators there?'

'The management have agreed to clear it for as long as we need it, but they've asked that we get there as early as possible. We'll have to get the girls up at dawn and do their make-up here before we leave.'

'So how do you plan to spend tomorrow?'

Casey shrugged. 'I really hadn't thought about it. Relax here by the pool, I suppose.'

'I thought of hiring a boat and going for a sail. Would you like to come with me?'

She gave him a quick glance and found his eyes fixed on her. Remembering what he'd said about being able to read her emotions, she hurriedly looked away. 'Who do you mean—all of us?'

'Don't be silly.'

A flush of colour came to her cheeks. 'You mean the three of us, then? You, Lucy and me?' she asked guardedly.

Ivo's lips twisted. 'Lucy is a very charming girl, but two days in her company are quite enough. I want to be with someone who can talk intelligently at my own level, with someone it gives me pleasure to look at and be seen with.'

'You ought to ask one of the model girls, then,' Casey said quickly, glancing at him from the corner of her eyes.

'I said intelligent; in the unlikely event of my ever wanting to go out with a clothes-horse, I'll ask one of them. But I don't happen to go for beauty without brains. I'm greedy; I like both—which is why I want to spend the day with you.'

Casey lowered her head, the rich silk fall of her hair hiding her face, but Ivo reached out a hand and lifted it away so that he could see her. 'You'll have to get out of that habit,' he reproved her.

'Will I?'

'Yes. You don't have to hide, Casey—not from me.'

His tone was gentle so that she couldn't get angry, but she didn't like the way he spoke to her, as if they were close, as if he had the right to make personal observations about her. She had only ever given one man that right and it wasn't something that she would give easily again. Finishing her drink, Casey stood up and said casually, 'Thanks for the drink—and for the invitation, but I don't think so.'

'You disappoint me,' Ivo remarked, leaning back in his seat. 'I thought you had more courage.'

She turned to face him, her back to the sun so that her hair was lit into a brilliant aureola around her head. 'Do me a favour, will you? Just don't think about me at all. OK?'

Ivo shook his head in one swift, negative movement. 'Sorry. That's impossible.' She looked at him for a moment and then moved to go, but Ivo said, 'Casey,' and she turned back reluctantly.

'Yes?'

'Lucy tells me you apologised to her. Thanks. I appreciate it.' She nodded, but he went on, 'I take it you no longer think that she and I are involved?'

Casey's chin came up and she looked at him contemplatively for a moment, at length saying, 'I think that Lucy is an innocent, yes.'

'Ah, so there's still a qualification where I'm concerned, is there?' He stretched his legs out in front of him and put his hands in the pockets of his shorts. 'You couldn't be more wrong, you know.'

'No, I don't know—and I don't really care,' she added deliberately.

She made to leave again, but Ivo said, 'Will you have dinner with me tonight?'

'With you—and all the others, yes.'

'Don't pretend to be obtuse, Casey. You know what I meant.'

'Possibly. But I can't seem to get my meaning across to you. I'm not interested, Ivo. I don't want to have dinner with you, or spend tomorrow with you, or anything else. So far as I'm concerned, you're just a business acquaintance and that's as far as it goes.'

She made to go on, but stopped in some alarm when Ivo got to his feet and stepped determinedly towards her, his eyes narrowing. She drew back, but came up against a wooden trellis hung with bougainvillaea that guarded the edge of the terrace and hid them from the people round the pool.

'So I'm nothing more than a business acquaintance, am I?' Reaching out, he put his arm round her waist and drew her towards him. 'And do you always tremble like this when other business acquaintances touch you? Or go rigid when they try to kiss you—like this?'

He bent his head, his lips seeking hers, but Casey put her hands against his chest, trying to push him away. 'No, don't.'

'You see?' He put his hand against her neck and found it taut and trembling. 'You let Ray Brent kiss you because it didn't mean a thing to you, did it? But with me it's different. We both know it's true, so you might as well admit it, Casey.'

He still had his arm round her waist and she found it difficult to think straight, but she said, 'No. I—I... That isn't so.'

'Liar,' he said, and nuzzled her neck.

'Don't.' Again she tried to push him away, but found that his strength was far greater than hers.

'Well, if you insist that you are immune to me, you can always prove it,' he said challengingly.

'What do you mean? How?'

'By having dinner with me tonight so that we can discuss—business.'

'What business?' she asked warily.

'Any you like. A deal for Decart to do two further calendars for Vulcan, perhaps.'

'That's bribery.'

'Well, of course it is. But you seem to expect the worst of me, so I might as well act that way,' Ivo said in exasperation.

There was the sound of voices and some holiday-makers walked up the steps to the terrace and came into view, making Ivo let her go, but he looked at her quizzically. 'Why not give yourself a chance, Casey?'

Herself? She thought it was an odd thing to say, but then wondered if he was right. It had been a long time since Mike had died, maybe it was time to see if she could experience any emotion other than grief again. But with Ivo Maine? She raised eyes that were suddenly cool and assessing to look at him, and he gave a theatrical shiver.

'Brrr. I've a feeling I'm being dissected.'

She continued to study him for a moment, thinking that she would be quite pleased to prove herself immune to him, then said, 'All right, I will have dinner with you.'

'And go sailing with me tomorrow?'

'I don't know yet.'

He gave a soft laugh. 'If I ever had any vain ideas about myself, you've certainly sent them crashing down. Will seven o'clock be OK?'

'Seven will be fine.' And she walked away, leaving Ivo to watch her go, his hands on his hips and a puzzled expression in his eyes.

Casey had second, third and fourth thoughts almost as soon as she reached her bungalow, and she would have given a lot to change her decision. She could imagine the reaction of the rest of the team when she and Ivo didn't turn up at Pedro's, and she was also worried that Lucy might have another 'joke' played on her. But that hadn't seemed to worry Ivo, and Lucy had to learn to stand on her own two feet some time. Besides, once bitten, twice shy—the girl would be careful what she drank from now on. But Casey still

wished she hadn't accepted Ivo's invitation. To choose
him to experiment on was stupid to say the least, when
she had been attracted to him from the start—and
still was, despite all her suspicions about him.

Nevertheless, she got ready carefully: washing her
hair, doing her make-up to suit the pale green dress
she'd chosen, and adding a light perfume that always
made Casey think of an English spring. By ten to seven
she was ready, and took a last look at herself in the
long mirror attached to the wardrobe door. She saw
a slim, sophisticated young woman who looked as if
she was completely in charge of her own life, her own
emotions. She tried to think back to how she had
looked about four years ago; a lot plumper certainly,
because she had been content then and had enjoyed
experimenting with cookery recipes, and they had en-
tertained and gone out to eat a lot at friends' houses
and at wine bars. And she had been more arty, her
hair long and her clothes of brighter colours. It was
only after she had gone into partnership with Steve
that she had become more tailored, more
businesslike, taking tips on dress and make-up from
the model girls she hired. And she had once been far
more outgoing and natural, warm and relaxed, and
supremely happy. But now she often felt like an empty
shell, as if there were nothing inside her that could
ever feel again. Her reflection in the mirror gave a
cynical little laugh; did Ivo really think he could make
her become a real human being instead of a robot
again? No, the risks and dangers were far too great.

At seven Ivo knocked on the door and Casey went
to open it. He was wearing black trousers and a white
dinner-jacket, and looked not only clean, but as if
he'd never been dirty. Casey had a sudden picture of

Mike dressed in torn jeans and an old shirt, his face and hands streaked with oil after lying under their first car for hours, trying to repair it, and she felt a prick of tears. To conquer them, her face drew into a tight, frozen mask as she desperately tried to fight the memory away. Not now, she prayed. Please not now. And she quickly locked her door and strode through the complex to the car park without greeting Ivo or even looking at him again.

He had hired an ordinary saloon car this evening, but the weather was still very warm and they drove with the windows open, the breeze catching Casey's hair and lifting it off her neck. Ivo drove out of Playa Blanca and headed north towards the interior of the island. The looming hulk of the Fire Mountains rose in the distance, the terrain between rock-strewn and pock-marked by small craters. In the mood she was in, Casey found the landscape grim and ominous; it made her feel that this was how the whole world would look if doomsday ever came. Lowering her head, she looked fixedly down at her lap where her hands were held tightly together. Ivo glanced at her several times, but saw the set look on her face and wisely refrained from making small talk.

He drove to Yaiza, a tiny town where the streets were laid out like those in a Spanish province, with palm trees casting shade in a central square, the houses whitewashed and very clean. They parked the car in a side street and walked to the square, past the fountain where a stone dolphin spilled an endless spray of water from its gaping mouth, and across to a café with tables set under the palm trees.

Ivo held a chair for her and said, 'I thought we might have an aperitif here before we go on to the restaurant.'

Casey nodded listlessly, fervently wishing she hadn't agreed to come out with him and wondering how soon she could decently plead a headache and cut the evening short.

The drinks came and Casey sipped hers and then sat back, looking round the square. It was pleasant here, she thought; already several of the local inhabitants had started to gather or to stroll about, taking their ease after the day's work was done. She wondered what it must be like to live here in such a small community where everyone knew everyone else, instead of a huge, uncaring city like London. She mused on the thought for a while, but then became aware of Ivo's eyes on her and reluctantly turned to face him.

'You'd be bored to death in a month,' he told her. 'You have too much drive ever to languish in a small place like this.'

Casey's eyes widened. 'How did you know what I was thinking?' she demanded uneasily.

He shrugged. 'It was simple enough; you had an extremely wistful look on your face.' He quirked an eyebrow. 'Not thinking that I could read minds or something, were you?'

'I was beginning to wonder.' She paused, then said with difficulty, 'Ivo, I really don't think this is a good idea. I'd like to go back after we've had this drink. I'm not very good company, and if you don't mind——'

'But I do mind,' Ivo interrupted.

'But we're here for all the wrong reasons,' she pointed out unhappily. 'At least, I am.' She paused and let her eyes rest on his face. 'But I don't really know your reasons, do I?'

Leaning forward, Ivo put his arms on the table and reached across to take her hand. She resisted him for a moment, but his grip was firm. 'My reasons,' he said, looking down at her hand and stroking the back of it with a long finger, 'are really very simple. I find you attractive, shiningly intelligent, mysterious, and very easy on the eye.' The little lines at the corners of his mouth creased as he added, 'Of course, I also find you stubborn, argumentative, open to prejudice and chauvinistic—but I still want to get to know you better.'

'I'm surprised there's anything left for you to know,' she answered, taken aback by his words.

She tried to draw her hand away, but Ivo held on to it and said, 'And now, how about telling me your reasons for coming out with me?' But Casey shook her head and wouldn't answer, so he said, 'All right, I'll tell *you* what they are. First of all you're off men, presumably because of this man who let you down. What did he do—walk out on you?' Casey's eyes had come up to meet his, wide and close to anger. She tried to wrench her hand away again, but Ivo said, 'Oh, no, you don't. You're going to listen. Where was I? Oh, yes—this guy who walked out on you. Well, he left you feeling very bitter and hurt, and you decided that you didn't want anything more to do with men in the future. Am I right?'

Casey gave him a glaring look. 'Have you finished?'

'No. I think that when you met me you felt some kind of attraction too, but you immediately began to fight it. And I think you came out with me tonight only to prove to yourself that you could resist me.'

Casey took a deep breath. 'Can I have my hand back now?' He released it, and she picked up her drink and took a long swallow. For several minutes she sat silently looking down at her glass, but then said honestly, 'Some of what you've said is true. I did—like you when we first met. But then, of course, there was Lucy.' She looked at him but he said nothing, just continued to watch her, so Casey looked away again and gave a short laugh. 'OK, maybe I did over-react about her because... Well, because.'

'Because you were jealous?'

She gave a decisive shake of her head. 'Sorry to prick your vanity, but no, I wasn't jealous. As a matter of fact I was glad, really, because it made me realise that—that I'd got my priorities right. But I felt sorry for Lucy.'

Ivo's eyebrows rose. 'Felt—not feel?'

The question made her frown, but then say almost in surprise, 'No, I—I don't think you are involved with her, or intend to be.' Looking into his eyes, she added slowly, 'I'm sorry.'

'So,' he said softly, 'an apology at last. *And* without an explanation. But what does it do for those priorities of yours, I wonder? Maybe you haven't got them right, Casey. Just because you were hurt once doesn't mean that...'

'Don't,' she said sharply. 'I've apologised, isn't that enough?'

'No. I'm beginning to think it isn't.' He paused, then, 'Don't you want to know why I insisted on you using Lucy as a model?'

She guessed where he was heading; if she said she was curious, then he would know that she was still interested in him, so, perversely, she said, 'No, not particularly.' And looked out across the square again.

Ivo sat back and picked up his drink. 'You were telling me why you agreed to come out with me tonight,' he reminded her.

'Was I? Yes, you were right; it was purely to prove to myself that—that . . .'

'That you could resist me,' Ivo supplied. She looked at him and he smiled suddenly. 'Poor Casey, it was so much easier to hate me, wasn't it? Tell you what— why don't we call a truce? Maybe we could even go back to the beginning, to the point where you decided that you liked me, for instance.' She looked at him uncertainly and he gave a crooked grin. 'Is that so hard?'

That grin was devastating. Casey caught her breath, realising that the test to prove her immunity was starting right now and with a vengeance. 'You can never go back,' she said positively. 'But, all right, I'm—I'm willing to try.'

'Good girl.' He gave another grin and then stood up. 'Come on, let's go and eat.' And taking her hand he led her out of the café.

The restaurant he had chosen was only a short walk away, through the square and along a street lined with pretty houses till they came to double ornamental gates with a discreet sign saying 'La Hacienda'. And that was exactly what the place was: a converted *hacienda* in the true Spanish manner, with a central courtyard around a double fountain, wooden beams and a big stone fireplace inside, friendly service and some of the most delicious food Casey had ever tasted. The

atmosphere, too, was warm and convivial; a guitarist
sat in a corner and softly played and sang old Spanish
folk-songs, the music haunting and gay by turns. They
drank rich cream sherry from the mainland and wine
made from grapes grown in the black volcanic ash of
Lanzarote, and slowly Casey began to unwind, to lose
the tension and to smile and talk with Ivo as they had
on that first day.

As the evening wore on the guitarist's songs became
louder and the diners, many of them locals, began to
clap to the music and join in the songs. There were
shouts of 'Manuel! Manuel!' and one of the waiters
abandoned the tray he was carrying and gave a spirited
rendering of *'La Bamba'*, putting everything he'd got
into it, to the delight of his audience. The musician
played louder and faster, until all they could do was
listen and applaud, the music filling their minds and
souls. Then the guitarist threw up his hands and refused to play another note, no more encores, no more
requests, no matter how much they pleaded and
cajoled.

Accepting that the evening was over, the diners reluctantly began to leave, their faces flushed with
warmth and wine, their spirits still full of music and
conviviality. Ivo and Casey left with the rest, walking
slowly back through the little town, the streets lit by
a full moon in a cloudless sky. Putting his arm round
her waist, Ivo drew Casey to his side and their footsteps became slower still. 'Tired?' he asked.

'Mm, a little, but pleasantly so. That was a wonderful evening, Ivo. Thank you,' she said sincerely.

'It was my pleasure. My very great pleasure.' He
came to a standstill and turned her to face him. They
had reached the square and stood beneath a palm tree,

its fringed leaves casting weird shadows across them in the moonlight. Ivo leaned against the trunk of the palm and, putting his hands on her arms, drew her towards him, his eyes intent. Immediately she became tense, ready to resist both Ivo and her own emotions. 'Relax,' he said softly. 'Whenever I touch you, you stiffen up. There's nothing to be afraid of.'

'But you only touch me when you're mad at me,' Casey pointed out, trying to change his mood.

'But I still want to touch you. I always have.' And he gently stroked her arms.

Casey tried to draw away. 'People will see us.'

'No, everyone's gone. Look around you.'

She did so and saw that the square was empty, all the diners having walked or driven away. It was very quiet, the only sound the soft sighing of the palm leaves in the gentle night breeze. But she still held herself away from him, her body stiff, and said, 'We ought to be getting back.'

'Why? There's no work tomorrow.' Putting his hands on her shoulders, Ivo let them slide down her back and on to her hips.

His fingers seemed to burn through the thin material of her dress, sending shock-waves of desire running through her. Desire? Was that what this was, this deep-down sensuousness that made her feel so restless and empty inside? It had been so long since Casey had felt like this that for a few moments she didn't recognise it. It's just frustration, she told herself—and heaven knew, she'd felt frustrated enough over the last years. But nothing had been as bad as this yearning ache, this need to be held and cherished and loved.

'Casey.' Ivo breathed her name against her neck. He kissed her lightly, his lips running over her skin, and drew her close to him, his hands still on her hips.

She held herself rigidly, fighting the burning need to move against him, the primeval instinct to rouse a man as only a woman can. Ivo's lips moved along her chin and found the corner of her mouth, touched it with tiny kisses, and explored the soft fullness of her lower lip with the tip of his tongue. A great tremor of awareness ran through her, impossible either to hide or control, and Ivo made a small sound deep in his throat as his mouth found hers and he kissed her fully for the first time.

It was only a kiss, Casey told herself. No different from when Ray had kissed her just a few nights ago. It would be either pleasant or unpleasant. It would last a couple of minutes and then it would be over, and she would know that she was still as immune to men as she had been since Mike had died. And she would be pleased because . . . A low moan broke from her as her senses started to spin, heat filled her body and she gasped, her mouth opening under his. Immediately his kiss deepened, became more passionate, and Ivo put his arms round her, holding her close and arching her against him. Panic seized her and Casey clamped her mouth shut and tried to push him away, but Ivo put his hand behind her head and went on kissing her, forcing her to surrender before his more dominant will.

She struggled, and when that didn't work began to curse him, making fierce, angry sounds against his mouth. But still he held her, his mouth becoming ever more importunate, and gradually her struggles lessened as Casey's senses began to swim again. This is what it must be like to drown, she thought, to float on this tide of sensuous pleasure and gradually be drawn down, down, even deeper, and never to come to the surface of reality again. To feel only these lips, these arms, this aching, unbearable yearning. A great, shuddering sigh shook her and she opened her mouth willingly at last, letting Ivo explore the soft interior, to touch her tongue lightly with his and make his own little sound of triumph at a battle won.

And when at last he lifted his head the triumph was still there in his eyes, but there was tenderness too. 'So you stopped fighting me at last,' he said softly.

'Yes, I—I suppose so.'

He nuzzled her neck and Casey tilted her head back, closing her eyes and letting awareness flood through her again. 'You see, there was nothing to be afraid of. You *were* afraid, weren't you?'

Lifting her hands, Casey put them on his shoulders and held him away from her, looking up into his handsome face, made leaner and sharper by the moonlight. 'No,' she said after a long moment. 'I don't think I was ever afraid of *you*. But I was terribly afraid of—of the way you made me feel.'

His eyebrows rising, Ivo said, 'And now?'

She gave a short, almost bitter laugh. 'Now I think I ought to be even more afraid,' she said unguardedly.

He gave her an intent look, but after a moment merely said, 'Then I shall just have to teach you not to be, won't I?' And he kissed her again.

They left the square shortly afterwards and drove home through the contorted land that looked even more tortured and extra-terrestrial in the moonlight. When they reached the complex, Ivo took Casey's hand and walked with her to her bungalow. There was no one about, the bar was closed and the pool covered, the residents either in bed or down at one of the bars in the village. As they walked along the path, Casey's heart began to pound; she was sure that Ivo would want to spend the night with her and she was ready to turn on him and tell him to go to hell. She should never have let him kiss her, never have succumbed to the emotions he seemed to be able to arouse in her so easily. A fierce surge of anger filled her and she took her hand from his, ready to do battle all over again.

In this belligerent mood she turned to face him when they reached her door, but was completely taken aback when he just said, 'Goodnight, Casey. Thanks for coming tonight; I can't remember when I've enjoyed an evening more.'

She stared at him, but then her anger evaporated as quickly as it had come and she said honestly, 'I haven't had such a good evening in ages, either.'

Picking up her hand, Ivo carried it to his lips, kissed it lightly and, still holding it, said, 'And will you come sailing with me tomorrow if I can hire a boat?'

'What about Lucy?' she prevaricated.

On a sudden note of irritation he said, 'To hell with Lucy, it's you I want to be with.'

Her eyes widened, but she was inwardly rather pleased at his vehemence. 'I don't know, I...' She looked into his eyes and suddenly all resistance melted again. 'Yes, all right, I'll come with you.'

'Good.' Putting his hands on her arms he drew her to him and gave her a brief, hard kiss. Then grinned at her and said, 'Goodnight, Casey. Be ready at eight.'

'Eight? But it's nearly two now. And you don't know if you can hire a boat yet.'

His grin grew devilish. 'I hired it yesterday—just in case.' And he gave her a wave as he turned and walked away.

The next day Casey felt almost like a schoolgirl playing truant. They left the complex early, before hardly anyone else was stirring, and she was filled with a great sense of giggling exhilaration, as if she were flinging off responsibilities and doing something wicked. They drove along the coast to the marina, where Ivo helped her aboard the boat. It was a smallish yacht with a minute cabin and dull red sails. Looking at it with some misgivings, she said, 'You do know how to handle this thing, don't you?'

'We-ell, it's been some time,' he said in a tone that was far from reassuring, but Casey soon found that Ivo was teasing her as he guided them surely out of the marina into the open sea.

It was time out. Casey leaned back against the side and felt the breeze lifting her hair and the sun on her face. She closed her eyes, listening to the ripple of the sea under their bow and the crack of the sail as it filled with wind. I can stand all this, she thought contentedly. A shadow passed in front of her and she opened her eyes to see Ivo looking down at her. He grinned and she smiled back without reserve, then felt fleetingly surprised at her own happiness.

They sailed across to the island of Fuerteventura, and anchored in a wide bay with a long, unbroken crescent of golden sand where they swam and then had a brunch meal. The beach was almost deserted, just a few people dotted around, in couples mostly.

'If this was Lanzarote, a beach as good as this would be swarming with people,' Ivo remarked.

'That's probably because there are lots of beaches here, and they're nearly all sand and not volcanic ash. And there aren't many tourists because there isn't enough water,' Casey informed him lazily. She had taken off her shorts and top, and lay stretched out on the planking of the deck in her bikini, soaking up the sun.

'Know-all,' Ivo taunted. He lay down beside her, propping himself up on one elbow, and traced a fingertip along her profile. When he reached her mouth, Casey went to bite him, but he was too quick for her. 'Minx.' He put his hand under her chin and bent to kiss her, a long, leisurely kiss that was soft and tender, not deepening into passion.

Casey let him kiss her, but didn't lift her arms to put them round his neck or touch him in any way. She was rather overwhelmed by his nearness in just a pair of shorts; he seemed so big, so strong, so arrantly masculine. He lifted his head and she opened her eyes to find him looking down at her intently. His hand was still under her chin and he brushed his thumb across her lips, then gently brushed her hair back from her face.

'You have such beautiful hair,' he murmured. 'It seems to flame in the sun.' Putting his hand on her waist, he began to kiss her exploringly, her eyes, her nose, her throat.

Casey's breath quickened as he moved his hand across her stomach caressingly, stroking her hot skin, making it hotter still. His lips found her mouth, and this time there was demand there, a demand she couldn't resist yet didn't entirely want to meet. Reaching up, Ivo tugged at the string of her bikini top and pulled it loose, then drew the scrap of ma-

terial down and began to explore her. Every nerve-
end seemed to come to life under his hand, thrusting
forward to meet the light, tantalising touch of his
fingers. Casey gave a low moan and clenched her fists
at her sides, almost hating him for what he was doing
to her, and yet unable to deny her body this hedon-
istic pleasure.

Ivo's breathing grew a little ragged and his kiss
hungered into passion. His hand wasn't so steady, so
assured, and she could feel the heat that grew in his
body. She began to tremble and Ivo lifted his head to
look down at her. She saw the desire in his eyes, naked
and dark, the tiny film of sweat on his upper lip. He
gazed at her for a moment, his features taut, but then
he moved his eyes downwards, openly admiring as he
went on fondling her. A spasm of awareness shook
her and he bent to kiss her breast. His lips closed over
her nipple, soft and infinitely sensuous. But Casey
gave a cry and suddenly jack-knifed away from him,
filled with terror at the emotions he aroused in her.
Without stopping to think, she went straight over the
side and let herself sink to the bottom, only slowly
turning to swim to the surface again and then strike
out for the shore.

She heard a splash behind her and was aware of
Ivo keeping pace with her, but she didn't look up at
him as she reached the shallows and walked up on to
the beach. There she retied her bikini with trembling
fingers and slowly turned to face him.

He was watching her, waiting for her to speak. She
bit her lip, then said tightly, 'I—I'm sorry, I'm not a
tease, if that's what you're thinking. It's just that—
that ...' She stopped, unable to go on.

'It's OK, I wasn't thinking that.' Ivo touched her arm reassuringly. 'Come on, let's go for a walk along the beach.'

But they didn't go far because they passed a group of people sunbathing on the sand and suddenly realised that they were all stark naked, men as well as women. Casey gave a startled gasp and punched Ivo in the ribs when he doubled up with laughter and said that he now knew why she'd been in such a hurry to get ashore. He chased her along the beach at that and, when he caught her, swung her up into his arms and carried her into the sea, threatening to duck her.

Casey squealed and pretended to struggle, but was shaking with laughter the whole time. 'All right, I won't duck you, but it will cost you.'

'Cost me what?'

'A kiss, of course.'

She pretended to consider the matter, but he got his kiss in the end, although he complained that it didn't really count because she was still laughing so much. It was good, that laughter, it made Casey feel about ten years younger, like a carefree teenager again. And they kept the atmosphere light for the rest of the day, Ivo telling her anecdotes and stories, often against himself, that amused her and gave her a greater insight into his character. She found him droll and witty, and the time just flew by in his company.

During the rest of that day he kissed her often but didn't attempt to let things go further, and Casey found that she began to look for the feel of his arm around her waist, the warmth of his closeness, and that heady feeling of excitement when his lips took hers.

It was early evening when they sailed back to Lanzarote, the dying sun setting the sea on fire and turning the sky to blood. Casey looked up at the sail and began to sing 'Red Sails in the Sunset' in soft contentment. Ivo grinned and joined in, his voice a pleasant baritone. They moored and walked along the waterfront to a café where they ate seafood and drank pink champagne, and it was late when they at last drew up in the car park by the complex.

Reaching over, Ivo put his arm round her shoulders and drew her closer. 'It's a shame we have to work tomorrow,' he said regretfully. 'We could have done this all over again.'

'Mm.' Casey nestled against his shoulder, feeling sleepy from so much wind and sea.

Lifting her face to meet his, Ivo kissed her nose and then sought her mouth in a kiss that sent the world whirling around her. 'Do you believe now that I was never interested in Lucy?' he murmured, when at last he raised his head.

After a kiss as devastating as that, Casey had no doubts at all. She took a deep breath, trying to steady her thumping heart. 'Why, yes, I——' She broke off and looked into his eyes, found that they were regarding her intently, and sat up straighter. 'Ivo,' she said in a completely different voice, 'just why *did* you insist on Lucy getting this job?'

CHAPTER SIX

Ivo gave a laugh that had more than a little triumph in it. 'I've been wondering when you'd get round to asking me that. I hope it means that you're starting to care.'

Casey hesitated, not wanting to commit herself. 'I think it just means that I can't contain my curiosity any longer,' she said lightly.

His mouth twisted wryly, but Ivo said, 'Well, at least that's something.' He settled himself more comfortably, his arm still around her, before he began his explanation. 'I've known Lucy and her family for several years,' he told her. 'Her father was the managing director of Vulcan Enterprises until his death last year, but we were also friends. We both used to play cricket and squash, and had more or less the same circle of friends. He made me one of the executors of his will, so I found myself acting as a sort of guardian for Lucy.'

'Is her mother dead too, then?' Casey asked.

'No, but she's one of those helpless sort of women who have always relied on a man to manage the practical side of their lives for them.' There was a disparaging note in Ivo's voice, and Casey gathered that he had little time for Lucy's mother. He went on, 'Of course, everyone on the board of directors at Vulcan was very fond of Jack Grainger, he was a marvellous person, and they all rallied round to help. When they found out that Lucy wanted to be a model, someone

121

came up with this calendar idea and I was given the job of putting it into operation.'

Casey's eyes widened as she raised her head from his shoulder to look at him. 'Good heavens! Talk about fools rushing in. I suppose they meant well, but trying to push her in at the top like this was the worst thing they could have done for her.'

'I know that now,' Ivo agreed ruefully. 'In fact, I did warn the board that I thought we ought to get some advice before we went ahead, but they were all so pleased that they'd come up with something that would help Jack's daughter that they wouldn't listen. We're not terribly *au fait* with the world of modelling in the City, you know.'

'So it seems. And they decided that you should go with Lucy and look after her, did they? Or was it your idea?'

'No, it was theirs. At first the board wanted Lucy's mother, Adele Grainger, to go with her as a chaperon, but Adele refused point blank. She had made other plans and no way was she going to change them.'

'She sounds terribly selfish,' Casey commented.

'Yes, she is. That's why we all wanted to do what we could for Lucy. So, as I was one of the executors of Jack's will, and because I was the nearest in age to Lucy, I was given the job of coming here to look after her.' He gave an ironic laugh. 'I was by no means happy about it at first. No way did I want to spend weeks acting as a glorified nursemaid to little more than a schoolgirl, but then—things changed.'

'They did? How?'

He gave her a lazy kind of smile, his eyes openly caressing. 'You walked into my office, of course.'

'Oh.'

'Quite.' He kissed her temple and then traced the line of her cheek with his lips, murmuring, 'You were like a shaft of sunlight on a winter's day. You dazzled me, took my breath away.'

'I would never have known,' Casey said, rather breathless herself. 'As I remember it, you were quite rude to me at first.'

'Panic reaction,' he told her. 'I was afraid of frightening you off if I let you see what an effect you'd had on me, so I went to the other extreme. I suppose it was that that made you take an instant dislike to me.'

'It didn't help,' Casey admitted. 'But—well, my first impression changed too.'

'It did?'

'Yes. I—after a while I began to like you. But then you insisted that Lucy must be one of the models.'

'And immediately jumped to the conclusion that I was some kind of a cradle-snatcher,' he finished for her, his mouth twisting.

Lifting a finger, Casey smoothed the lines from his mouth. 'It was hardly surprising. A lot of men go for very young girls.'

'But I don't happen to be one of them.' He caught her hand when she went to take it away, and held it so that he could kiss her fingers and then gently bite the soft flesh.

'So what kind of girl do you like?' Casey couldn't resist asking.

Ivo smiled. 'That's a question I've been waiting all my life to find the answer to. And I'm only just finding out that I like them with flaming red-gold hair and soft green eyes that look sad when they think no one's watching, that flash like green ice in the sun when they're angry, but transform into breathtaking beauty when they give one of those smiles that they really mean. One of their special smiles.' And he gently kissed the corner of her mouth before he raised his head again and went on, 'And I like a girl who walks with her head held high as if defying all the world, whose voice is as soft as music, and with a body so beautiful I ache to hold and touch her. Who's basically kind and loving, but is scared to show it because she's been hurt and is afraid of loving again.'

His description came to an end, but Casey couldn't find anything to say. She turned her head and lowered it so that her hair hid her face. She felt strangely humble, a feeling she hadn't experienced since Mike had told her he loved her and wanted to marry her. But Ivo was right, she was scared, scared as hell.

'You're hiding again,' he remonstrated, and put his hand under her chin so that she had to turn and look at him. 'What are you thinking?'

'That you're right, that I am afraid.'

'What happened with this other man, Casey? Were you in love with him?' She straightened up and drew away from him, immediately on the defensive against this intrusion into her privacy, but Ivo held her and said urgently, 'Don't shut me out, Casey. Can't you see that I want to know everything about you? I want to share with you, your past as well as your future. I——'

'You want too much,' she cut in harshly, then bit her lip and added more gently, 'I'm sorry, I can't— can't talk about it.'

He looked at her closed face for a moment, then said stiffly, 'I'm rushing you. I'm sorry.'

'Yes, you are.' But she suddenly smiled and turned to him. 'Look, today's been great. Don't let's spoil it. And we have a busy day tomorrow, so I really think we ought to go in, don't you?'

'No, but I have a feeling that you're going to insist.'

He let her go reluctantly and came round to open her door for her. The breeze had increased, bringing the smell of the sea as they walked through the complex.

'How about coming for a dip in the sea tomorrow morning?' Ivo suggested.

'Yes, I should like that. It will have to be early, though.'

'Fine. We might even get the beach to ourselves.'

They reached her bungalow and Casey turned to face him. 'Thank you for a wonderful day.'

She half proffered her hand, but Ivo brushed it aside as he took her into his arms and kissed her demandingly, moulding her body against his own, his hold gradually tightening as passion increased. 'I don't want to leave you,' he said thickly when at last he raised his head.

Casey didn't answer or look at him. Her heart was thumping, but every nerve-end was on edge, waiting to deny him when he asked to go to bed with her. But he must have felt her tension and understood it, because Ivo gave a short sigh and stepped back. 'Goodnight, Casey. I'll call for you at seven tomorrow morning.' And he raised his hand in salute as he turned and walked briskly away.

Casey didn't go to sleep for some time. Her mind dwelt on the weekend; she had enjoyed herself so much, more than she had ever thought it possible to again. And she had enjoyed Ivo's kisses too. Too much. A great sense of guilt filled her, but she pushed it away.

They were only kisses, for heaven's sake. OK, so Ivo fancied her, and maybe she was beginning to fancy him too, but she had never gone in for casual sex and she wasn't about to start now. And Ivo was a civilised man; if she said no, that's enough, he wouldn't force himself on her. He wouldn't like it, of course, but he would have to accept that she didn't want an affair with him.

She lay back on the pillow, gazing at the darkened room, trying to convince herself of this, but suddenly thought: Who are you trying to fool? The way Ivo had spoken, the way he had kissed her and looked at her, those weren't the actions of a man who would accept no for an answer. Not forever. He might now, of course, because they hadn't known each other for very long, but if she went on letting him kiss her the way she had today, then he was entitled to expect more than that before very long. The thought frightened her. She shouldn't have gone out with him, shouldn't have let him touch her. Because she didn't want to make that kind of commitment, not now, not ever.

It was late before she fell asleep, and she gave a reluctant moan when Ivo banged on her door the next morning. 'Go away,' she groaned.

'Wake up, sleepyhead, you wanted to go swimming.'

Cursing her own folly, Casey went to the door and unlocked it before hurrying back to her bedroom to wash and dress. Ivo came in and had a cup of coffee ready for her when she joined him ten minutes later. He looked at her and grinned. 'You'll feel much better when you've had a swim. I didn't think you were one of those people who hated getting up in the mornings.'

'I'm not usually. I—I didn't sleep very well.'

He gave her a searching look. 'Too much on your mind?' She nodded and he said, 'Not worrying about the shoot, are you?'

'No, it's going OK. Quite well, really.'

'It must be me, then.'

She took a long swallow of her coffee. 'That feels better. Why don't we go and have that swim?'

Ivo's left eyebrow rose. 'Dodging the issue, Casey?'

Setting down her cup, she gave him an over-bright smile. 'Of course. It's much too early in the morning. Come on, I'll race you down to the beach.'

Casey ran out of the bungalow with Ivo close behind, and they got a startled look from one of Chas's assistants who was just coming out of his own bungalow across the other side of the pool. But the surprise changed to a knowing look, and he lost no time in telling the rest of the team what he'd seen, so that by the time they were ready to leave for the day's shoot they all believed that Casey and Ivo had spent the night together. Even Lucy had heard the gossip, and it was her blush when she went to speak to her that alerted Casey to what had happened.

She ignored Lucy's blush just as she ignored all the *double entendres* and sly remarks that came her way that day. She didn't like it, but she certainly didn't intend to add fuel to the fire by making any denials. Ivo cottoned on almost as quickly as she did, and gave her a ruefully expressive glance. After that, Casey expected him to keep away from her, and wasn't at all pleased when he made a point of singling her out and putting a casual arm on her shoulder or round her waist whenever he came over to talk to her. Because it was so casual, she couldn't openly object; it was no more than Chas or Ray would do when she

talked to them, but all the same she didn't like it—
Ivo's touch put her off her work, whereas the other
men's didn't. And it just made everyone believe that
the gossip was true, of course.

Today they were shooting in a grotto towards the
north of the island and using all the models, so Lucy
was naturally excited. The grotto was like a huge open-
ended cave filled with a pool of still, green water and
just a narrow path along its edge. The place was
heavily commercialised, one end of it having been
turned into a nightclub with tiers of tables, a dance-
floor and a bar, which they had to screen off before
they could shoot. But the shots worked very well, with
Ray—who had a marvellous physique—dressed as a
water god, and the girls draped around him. Ray's
costume was very cleverly done, just a G-string dis-
guised by tendrils of fake weeds that curled around
his bare legs and torso. The girls were in similar costumes, their hair sleeked back from their heads and
their bodies covered in green make-up so that they
looked as if they melted into the water. They were
almost naked, the aim of the calendar being to attract
attention, but Casey saw to it that Lucy's tendrils of
weed covered her in all the right places.

They only had a limited time to shoot before the
grotto opened to the public, so there was no time for
rehearsals or nervousness. Lucy was briskly told where
to go and what to do and, because Casey took it for
granted that she would do it right, the young girl just
did as she was told and posed beautifully. So for once
everything went right and they were finished by the
time the first eager spectators came into the cavern.

Casey had hoped to finish off the shoot they had
had to abandon on Friday, but it took so long to get

the make-up off the girls and wash their hair that the place was full of tourists again by the time they got there in the late afternoon.

'Why don't you create a diversion to draw the spectators away?' Ivo suggested, coming up to Casey and putting a familiar arm around her waist as they stood beside the coach. 'We could drive the bus round to the other side of the hill and set up a fake shoot while Chas stays here with the minimum people he needs to take the real photographs.'

'Great idea,' Chas enthused. 'Let's do it.'

'Casey?' Ivo looked at her questioningly when she didn't speak.

'Yes, I agree. It's a very good idea.' But her face was set and she deliberately stepped away from his hold, making Ivo look at her keenly.

The diversion worked well and they were able to take the shots they wanted, the setting sun making a brilliant background to the fire mountain. Pleased with the day's work, they drove home, tired and hungry, all óf them more than ready to head for Pedro's and dinner.

As they walked down through the village, Casey made a point of talking to Chas, and of sitting next to him at the restaurant, but the others took it for granted that she would want to sit next to Ivo and left the seat on her other side vacant. He came to take the seat, but she turned away and concentrated on discussing the next day's shoot with Chas until even the photographer could find nothing more to say and turned to his other neighbour.

Ivo had been talking to Lucy who was sitting on his right, but now he turned and looked at Casey's averted profile. Her right hand was lying on the table and he put his over it, but she jerked her hand away as if it had been stung and put it in her lap. Ivo's face hardened but he didn't say anything until they left the restaurant; then, before Casey could tag along with someone else, he put a firm hand under her elbow and said, 'Let's take a walk.'

She resisted momentarily, but then let him lead her down to the beach, away from the others who were mostly making for the bar. When they were far enough away from the restaurant, Ivo sat down on the seawall and pulled her down beside him. 'OK, so why the cold shoulder?' he demanded.

'You know why; they think—they're under the impression that...'

'That we're lovers,' Ivo finished for her. 'Is it so hard to say? And what the hell does it matter what they think?'

'It matters,' Casey returned angrily.

'Why?' She didn't answer and he said shortly, 'Are you afraid it will undermine your authority over them or something?'

'No.' Casey shook her head unhappily. 'I—I don't want them to gossip about me. When you saw that they'd jumped to the wrong conclusion you should have kept away from me, but you kept coming up and touching me as if you owned me, as if you had the right to... As if we really were—involved.'

'As far as I'm concerned, we *are* involved,' Ivo said bluntly.

'No, we're not,' she corrected sharply. 'Not in the way they think.'

'No.' He paused, then added deliberately. 'Not yet.'

Casey's face flamed and she got quickly to her feet, but Ivo caught her before she'd gone a yard and held on to her arm. 'And we won't be involved in that way until you want it.' She swung round to stare at him, searching his face as he went on, 'But I'm not going to pretend that I feel nothing for you. I want to be close to you, I want to touch you, and I don't care who knows it. I'm not ashamed of the way I feel about you. Are you?'

'No, I . . .' She hesitated, at a loss. His openness made Casey feel small and mean, but she was also full of a terrible sense of guilt, as if she were being unfaithful to Mike's memory. 'I'm not sure how I feel about you,' she admitted.

'Aren't you?' Ivo drew her to him and put his hand up to her face. 'But you enjoyed going out with me?'

'Yes.'

'And you liked it when I kissed you?' he said, his voice thickening.

Casey stiffened and her answering 'Yes' came out reluctantly.

Putting his arm round her, he drew her closer and kissed her neck, then began to stroke her arm, his touch on her bare skin soft and caressing. Casey trembled and he smiled and said, 'And you always tremble just like that whenever I touch you, so there's no use pretending, Casey. You can't hide from the truth. You're as sexually aware of me as I am of you.'

'No, I . . .' She put her hands up to resist him, but Ivo put his hand in her hair and kissed her fiercely, his hungry lips demanding and getting the passionate response he wanted.

'Yes,' he insisted.

Casey opened drowned green eyes and looked up at him, her lips still parted sensuously. 'Yes,' she admitted on a soft sigh.

He kissed her again, his hand going to her breast, but presently he raised his head. 'I know you've been hurt, Casey, and I'm not going to rush you. But I'm not going to let you deny what we have between us. I want you. I want to take you to bed and love you. But not for just a night or a brief affair. When I take you to bed I want it to mean a great deal to both of us. I want it to be a beginning, not an end. Do you understand? Do you?' he demanded urgently.

'Yes.' She looked up into his face, seeing the strength and purpose there in his eyes, in the determined set of his chin. She had been right, he wasn't a man who would go on taking no for an answer, but he would give her time, and for the moment she seized on that and put off thinking of the future. She felt secure in his promise, safe enough to go on as they were, enjoying the reawakening femininity that his kisses and caresses had brought to life, and able to stifle the feelings of guilt. Mike would want her to be happy, she told herself. He would want her to go on living even though he was dead, but something in her had died with Mike, and within her now was a great fear which, although she could temporarily bury it, would never go away.

Relying on Ivo's promise not to rush her, Casey was able to relax and accept it when he acted as if they were a twosome in public, often kissing her lightly as well as putting his arm around her. She had been worried that Lucy might have a schoolgirl crush on Ivo without him knowing it, but Lucy seemed pleased by the situation and confided to Casey that she had never seen Ivo nuts over a girl before, and she thought it was about time he met someone gorgeous enough to floor him.

'What a way to describe it,' Casey laughed. 'But thanks for the compliment.'

'My mother is always trying to match him up with one of her friends,' Lucy went on. 'But they're mostly divorced and not his type at all. He's usually terribly polite, and you know he's bored. Was he polite with you at first?'

Casey shook her head. 'Definitely not. He was rude from the first moment I met him.'

'There you are, then,' Lucy exclaimed triumphantly. 'He's obviously crazy about you.' She gave Casey a sideways look. 'But then you must know that, if you and Ivo are——'

'We're not,' Casey interrupted firmly, and stood up. 'For heaven's sake, Lucy, I've only known him a few months.'

'I thought people didn't need very long nowadays.'

'Well, you thought wrong. There's no need to rush into a relationship, Lucy. Remember that when you meet someone you like. The kind of man who thinks of nothing but getting you into bed with him isn't the loving and caring kind. OK?'

'OK.' Lucy grinned. 'But don't think I don't know that you just changed the subject.'

Casey laughed, realising that the younger girl had grown up a lot in the last couple of weeks. She got on well with the rest of the team now because she had a naturally happy disposition and was willing to learn, and they had let up on her once they realised that she wasn't Ivo's girlfriend.

The shoot was going well, too, and Casey's only problem at the moment was her cousin, Tina, who was going through a sticky patch in her marriage and kept telephoning to tell her all about it. Casey had

had to call her cousin because she felt that it was unfair for Steve to be burdened with relaying all her messages, and once Tina had got the complex number she phoned nearly every night. Casey listened as patiently as she could, but got really annoyed when Tina informed her that she had left her husband and moved into Casey's flat. But at this distance there was little that Casey could do, although she resolved to have it out with her cousin as soon as she got back to England.

During the next week or so her relationship with Ivo strengthened in that they talked a great deal, discovering each other's likes and dislikes, finding things like the love of music and art that they had in common, and other things in which they were violently opposed and had heated discussions over. That the discussions usually ended by Ivo pulling her into his arms and silencing her with his mouth, kissing her until she forgot everything but the aching awareness of her own body, only added to the spice of the argument. He didn't attempt to make love to her, but his kisses grew hungrier, his caresses more intimate and urgent, and she could feel his heart thudding in his chest when he pulled himself away from her, his hands balled into tight fists.

They had been in Lanzarote for almost three weeks, and the calendar shoot was well under way, when they returned to the complex after an early swim in the sea one morning and Ivo was called to the telephone. Casey waited for him outside the reception area and knew it was bad news as soon as she saw the grim look on his face.

'There's a crisis at Vulcan. Somebody wants to take over one of our subsidiaries, and they want me to go and deal with it. I'll have to fly back today, I'm afraid.'

'Today?' Casey looked up at him, surprised by her feeling of dismay.

Ivo took her hand. 'Come and help me pack.'

She went with him to his bungalow, but when they reached it he took her into his arms and kissed her compulsively. 'Hell, Casey, I don't want to leave you. Not now, not when we're becoming so close.'

His hair was still damp and she could taste salt from the sea on his lips. Putting her hands on his shoulders, she clung to him, feeling the thrust of his hips as Ivo held her close. She moved against him and he groaned, his grip tightening as he held her.

'Will it take long?' Casey asked raggedly. 'Will you be able to come back before the shoot ends?'

'Do you want me to?'

She looked up at him, saw the intent look in his eyes and realised what his question implied. But he was holding her so close against him that she was filled with an overpowering ache of yearning, a longing so deep that everything else was forgotten as she said huskily, 'Yes. Yes, I want you to come back.'

'Darling.' Ivo kissed her again, but then gave a groan of frustration as he straightened up. 'I must pack. Marilyn has booked me a flight on this morning's plane, and if I don't hurry I'll miss it.'

'I'll pack while you change,' Casey offered.

'Thanks.' He sorted out some clothes and disappeared into the bathroom to shower.

Taking his case from the wardrobe, Casey began to pack his things, carefully folding his shirts as Mike had taught her. Her hands stilled as Casey stared down

at the case, Mike's face vivid in her mind. She dropped
the shirt she was holding, recoiling from it, just as
Ivo called out to her through the partly open bathroom
door.

'What—what did you say?' she managed.

'I said that it will probably be best if you pack
everything, just in case I can't get back.' Ivo came
out of the bathroom and smiled at her. 'But I'm certainly going to move heaven and earth to try.'

'Please, you mustn't—mustn't neglect your work.
I'm sure they wouldn't have sent for you if it wasn't
serious,' Casey said on a sudden note of panic.

But Ivo was in too much of a hurry to notice it.
Going to the mirror, he knotted his tie and grimaced
at his reflection. 'This is the first time in my life I've
been reluctant to face a challenge or get back to work.
How much longer do you think you'll need to complete this shoot?'

'Only a week at the most. It really wouldn't be
worth while for you to try to get back, so please don't
bother to——'

'Even to see you for a few hours would be worth
it,' Ivo cut in, coming to put his hands on her
shoulders. Then he grinned. 'Hey, I thought you were
supposed to be packing for me. What happened, did
you have your mind on other things?'

There was a teasingly suggestive note in his voice,
but Casey looked away as she said, 'Yes, I—I suppose
I did.'

Ivo laughed before finishing the packing himself,
quickly and efficiently. Then he kissed her again,
saying, 'Lord, I'm going to miss you, Casey. But I'll
phone every day. Explain to Lucy for me, will you?
And say goodbye to the others. I *must* go, my taxi

will be here by now. Goodbye, darling, think about me when I'm gone.' Pulling her into his arms, he took her lips in a brief, urgent kiss of frustrated yearning, then tore himself away, grabbing up his case and hurrying through the complex.

Casey went to the door and watched him go. At the path leading to the car park Ivo turned and waved and she slowly lifted her hand, but he was gone before she could wave back. She stared at the empty path, her feelings a crazy mixture of apprehension and relief, fear that she might have committed herself to something she wasn't ready to face, and the uncertain hope that Ivo might not be able to get back so that she wouldn't have to face it after all.

The calendar shoot went ahead, but two days later the sky darkened and it rained solidly for three days, making any work impossible. The team amused themselves as best they could, but it gave Casey many long hours to realise what she had quickly come to suspect—that she was missing Ivo a great deal. At first she found it almost impossible to believe that she could miss him so quickly or so much, but the days felt long and empty without him to talk to, argue and laugh with, or to listen to as he talked knowledgeably from his own experience. And she also missed his physical closeness, the weight of his hand on her shoulder or his arm round her waist. And his kisses, which she had been half afraid to accept—now she longed for them desperately.

True to his promise, Ivo rang every evening, often quite late, after they had returned from Pedro's, and although he didn't say very much about the take-over bid Casey guessed that he was working extremely hard to settle it. He told her how much he missed her and longed to see her again, his words as warm as a caress, each endearment as exciting as a kiss. At first Casey found it hard to voice how she felt in return, just as she had never gone into his arms and kissed him of her own accord. It had always been Ivo who had kissed her, who had instigated everything. But as the empty days passed her voice became warmer and, perhaps because he was so far away, she was able to tell him that she missed him too.

Because of the bad weather the shoot carried over to another weekend, but they finished the final shots at last on Saturday afternoon, and that night they all went down to the bar in the village to celebrate. Casey went along too, having told Ivo she wouldn't be in the complex to take his call that evening. He had told her to buy everyone champagne on him and that he would call her at her flat when she got back to England on the following Monday. Casey had mixed feelings about that; one part of her longed to see him, but the other was afraid of the decision Ivo was soon going to force her to make.

The weather was baking hot to compensate for so much rain, and they all sat at tables outside on the pavement. Ivo's champagne was soon drunk, as were the bottles that Casey bought on behalf of Decart, so Chas bought some too. Spanish champagne was much cheaper than the real French stuff, but tasted equally potent, and they were soon all feeling distinctly happy, laughing and dancing out under the stars. Casey danced with all the men, but had just started a slow number with Chas because he said that was all he could manage, when someone came up behind him out of the darkness, tapped him on the shoulder, and said, 'Please excuse me, Chas, but I've come a long way for this dance.'

'Ivo!' Casey stared up at him in amazement as Chas grinned and moved to make way for the other man. 'But you're—you're supposed to be in England.'

'No,' he assured her. 'I'm most definitely here.' And he took her in his arms and kissed her deeply, right there in front of everyone.

Casey was so surprised and pleased to see him that she returned his kiss ardently, forgetting about the audience for several long moments. Then she remembered and pushed Ivo away laughingly. But there was tension mingled with the laughter, because his kiss had been that of a man who didn't intend to wait any longer. Compelling and urgent, it told of a hunger that had to be appeased, of a need that seethed beneath the outward surface of civilised control. Glancing up into his face, Casey saw the hunger revealed naked in his eyes. She flushed and, quickly turning away, called out, 'Hey, Lucy, look who's here.'

'I saw him.' Lucy laughed and ran over to give Ivo a hug. 'Fancy coming all this way. Didn't you know that we've finished the shoot? We're all going home on Monday.'

'Yes, I knew,' Ivo replied. He turned to look at Casey and held her gaze. 'But I couldn't think of anywhere I'd rather spend the weekend.'

As Casey looked at him, she realised that the moment of decision had come, that he had come back to claim her now, tonight. She lowered her head, her heart thumping painfully, but she felt his eyes still on her compellingly, and knew that he was waiting for

an answer. Slowly she raised her head and tried to
smile, but there was an underlying tremor of apprehension in her voice as she said huskily, 'I'm—I'm
glad you came back.'

CHAPTER SEVEN

Ivo smiled and, drawing her into his arms, began to dance. He didn't say anything, for which Casey was thankful, but then words were unnecessary now; she had said everything he wanted to hear when she welcomed him back. The music ended and they strolled over to where the rest of the team were sitting, Ivo's arm around her waist possessively. He was greeted by the others, most of them with grinning, knowing looks. They all know why he's here, Casey thought in a sudden moment of panic. They'll talk about us when they get home. She made an instinctive movement away from him, but Ivo's hold tightened and he looked down at her with such an understanding grin that suddenly everything was all right again.

What does it matter if they talk? she thought. Who is there who would really care? Fleeting pictures of her own family and Mike's went through her mind, but she pushed them aside. She must live her own life, try and find happiness if she could. And Ivo made her happy, life seemed worth living again now that she had met him. But would she still be happy with him once she had committed herself to him completely? She knew that he wanted her, but for how long? He had paid her many compliments and said that he cared for her, that she'd knocked him off his feet, but Ivo had never said that he loved her. Uncertainty hit her again because Casey knew that, once

she went to bed with him, for her the commitment
would be total. If he tired of her she would feel both
hurt and cheap. Especially after Mike. But she mustn't
think of Mike, not tonight.

Slipping from Ivo's hold, Casey went over to where
she'd been sitting and picked up her glass, drinking
down the champagne as if she were very thirsty. The
music began again and she finished her dance with
Chas while Ivo danced with Lucy. They passed each
other as they moved around the impromptu dance-
floor and Ivo gave her a lazy smile, willing to wait
now, confident that they would be lovers before the
night was over. Casey turned away, her heart
thumping, knowing that she couldn't deny him, but
terribly afraid of what the future might bring. But
suddenly a solution came to her and she felt almost
giddy with relief; maybe there was a way that this terrible hunger could be appeased which would give her
peace of mind too.

The party went on until the early hours, but after
he'd been there only an hour or so Ivo drew Casey
close to him as they danced. He kissed the lobe of her
ear, making her squirm with pleasure, and murmured, 'Why don't we take a walk along the beach?'

She looked up, her pulses immediately beginning
to race, and faltered, 'All—all right.'

It was surprising how quickly the noise and lights
from the bar faded. The tide was out and they took
off their shoes and walked on the soft sand at the
edge of the sea, the noise of the waves breaking on
the shore and rippling across the beach making much
more gentle music. Soon it felt as if they were in
another world, the distant lights from the bar the lights
of another land. Darkness and moonlight enfolded

them in their soft embrace as Ivo drew her to him and kissed her in growing passion, his lips finding her eyes, her throat, and returning with hungry intensity to her lips. 'Oh, Casey, my darling girl. If you only knew how much I've missed you. How much I've been longing to hold you in my arms again like this. Hold you, kiss you, love you.' He felt her tremble and looked into her face. 'Did you miss me, Casey? Did you?'

'Yes. I—I told you.'

His eyes glittered down at her, his face tense with desire, then he pulled her almost roughly against him, holding her low down on her waist as he kissed her, letting her know how much he wanted her. Casey put her arms round his neck, losing herself in his kisses, deliberately letting go of her senses and thinking of nothing but the leaping excitement in her veins and the growing urgency of her body as he held her close, so close, but not close enough.

His breathing was ragged and his heart hammering in his chest as Ivo raised his head at last. 'Let's go back.'

She nodded, unable to speak, and Ivo led her through the village, asleep under the starlit night, the square white houses looking like sugar-cubes thrown down by a giant hand and scattered across the earth. The holiday complex was quiet when they reached it, the only lights the miniature lampposts illuminating the pathways and the underwater lights in the pool that gave the water the weird, luminous look of phosphorescence.

They reached Casey's bungalow and Ivo went up the pathway, drawing her along beside him. His arm was round her waist and she could feel his body against the length of hers. 'The key,' he murmured, and bent to kiss her cheek, trailing his mouth along her jawline to her lips.

Casey fumbled in the pocket of her skirt and found the key, but her hands were so unsteady that she couldn't get it in the lock. Taking it from her, Ivo opened the door and drew her inside, then closed it and turned off the porch light.

'Casey.' He repeated her name with growing intensity, holding her face in his hands as he kissed her with a passion that he no longer had to hold in check. His shoulders hunched as he rained kisses on her face, murmuring words of need and passion, his body beginning to shake in anticipation. Still kissing her, he picked her up and carried her into the bedroom, the uncurtained window casting a rich shaft of moonlight across the bed. 'I want you so much,' he breathed. 'These days that I've been away from you have driven me mad, thinking of you, longing for you. I couldn't get you out of my mind.'

He set her down on her feet and she put her arms round his neck, letting him kiss and caress her, her breath catching in her throat as Ivo's hands went to the buttons on her blouse and he began to undo them. The last button was undone and he put his hands inside, his touch burning hot on her skin as he encircled her waist, then gently drew his hands upwards to her shoulders and pushed the blouse off and down her arms, letting it drop to the floor. He kissed her neck and she tilted her head back, her eyes closed in heady pleasure as he explored the long column of her throat; then he found the clasp of her bra, undid it, and drew off the wispy pieces of black lace.

He drew back, looking his fill, before he lifted his hands to cup her firm breasts. Casey gasped and shuddered, gasped again as his fingers began to fondle her, the nipples hardening as desire racked her and every nerve-end came flamingly alive. She put her hands on his shoulders, her nails digging into him as she moved under his hands, such knowledgeable hands that knew exactly how to rouse her senses to fever pitch. Ivo kissed her fiercely, then, taking his mouth from hers, he lowered his head to her breasts. A cry broke from her lips and Casey put her hands on his head, her breath gasping moans of pleasure. When she couldn't stand it any longer, her insides on fire with frustration, she tore herself from his hold. She stood gasping, her body quivering, but made no demur when Ivo unzipped her skirt and let it fall to the floor. She stepped out of it and kicked off her shoes, then stood in frozen stillness as he knelt to take off the last piece of lace. He rose very slowly, his hands caressing the length of her slim figure, but once upright he pulled her close against the masculine hardness of his body as he kissed her with fierce, hungry passion.

Then, his hands trembling, Ivo lifted his head and took hold of her hands, raised them to his own shirt. Casey undressed him slowly, exploring him as she did so, running her fingertips along the steel-like muscles of his arms, across the breadth of his shoulders, and circling them around his tiny nipples that were nevertheless as sensitive as hers. There was sweat on Ivo's skin and she could feel his heart pounding even before she'd reached his waist, and afterwards his hands gripped her arms, hurting her as he pulled her suddenly towards him, taking her mouth in uncontrolled longing.

Picking her up, he carried her over to the bed and laid her on it, stood looking down at her, clothed in silver by the moonlight. 'If you only knew how much I've longed for this moment,' he said hoarsely. 'How I've ached to see you like this, to touch you and love you.'

She stared up at him, her body trembling, unable to move or to speak, her green eyes wide and vulnerable.

'My darling.' Ivo lowered himself on to the bed beside her. He stroked her face gently as he looked at her, then slowly began to explore her body with his hands and his mouth, murmuring words of love that merged into one long caress.

Casey didn't hear the words, only the tender, intimate tone of his voice that soon became hoarse and unsteady, thick with desire and excitement. His touch, his lips and his tongue, and the consummate skill with which he used them to arouse her, carried Casey to the edge of ecstasy. She cried out, the emptiness inside her yearning desperately for fulfilment, her body in a ferment of excitement. Ivo's skin was so hot, she could feel it burning against her as he raised himself over her, his breath rasping in his throat.

'Casey, oh lord, Casey, I'm crazy about you.'

He came down on her, taking her mouth as he did so, wanting to be close to every intimate part of her. Casey gave a moaning cry and raised her arm to put it round him, but they had moved nearer the edge of the narrow bed and her hand caught something on the bedside-table and sent it crashing to the floor. There was the sound of breaking glass that instantly cut through passion and desire and made her suddenly grow rigidly still as she realised what it was.

'Mike! Oh, no!'

Casey groaned out his name as his memory came flooding back and she instinctively began to fight Ivo, pushing him away, struggling out from under him, hitting out at him in a frenzy of loathing. 'Get away from me! Damn you, let me go!'

She broke free from his startled, disbelieving hold and rolled on to the floor, cutting her hands and knees on the broken glass. But Casey didn't feel any pain. She scrabbled among the jagged pieces on the floor for the photograph, found it, then got to her feet and began to pull on her clothes haphazardly.

'What is it? Casey, was I hurting you? What is it, darling?' Trying to drag himself back to reality from intense passion, Ivo groped for the light switch in the unfamiliar room, but by the time his unsteady hand had found it Casey had pulled on her clothes and was making for the door, the photograph in her hands and tears running down her cheeks.

'Wait! Casey, wait!' He sprang off the bed and came after her, but she eluded him and ran out of the bungalow, leaving the door wide open behind her.

She ran through the empty night with no clear idea where she was going, but instinct took her down to the sea and along to where the seats were built into the wall. She cowered there, holding Mike's picture tightly to her breast, keening over it in an agony of terrible remorse and grief. Tears filled her eyes and her body was racked with great sobs that she couldn't stifle. She felt so ashamed, so dirty, overcome with guilt.

Footsteps echoed along the promenade, coming steadily and unhesitatingly nearer in swift, purposeful strides. They climbed the steps and then Ivo stood before her, his face dark with scarcely suppressed anger. 'I thought I'd find you here,' he said grimly. 'This is your bolt-hole, isn't it? The place you come to when you're too much of a coward to face up to things.'

Casey raised her head to look at him, but then shuddered and said miserably, 'Go away. Leave me alone.'

'Leave you alone? Hell, I ought to knock your head off for what you did.' With a sudden lunge Ivo grabbed hold of her and yanked Casey to her feet.

She had no real fear of him, in fact she wasn't thinking of Ivo at all, only of Mike and the way she had betrayed his memory. She was suffused with guilt and just wanted to be left alone with this anguish that was tearing her apart. So her tone was irritated more than anything as she said, 'Let go of me. I don't want you. I——'

Casey's words were cut off as Ivo began to shake her in a rage of anger. 'Damn you, do you have any idea what you just did to me? Do you? You selfish little bitch! To lead me on and then duck out when you did!'

'No, it wasn't like that.' He was still shaking her, his fingers biting into her arms, but Casey put up her hands to hold him off. 'It wasn't like that, I tell you,' she yelled at him.

He became still, his body trembling, his mouth contorted as Ivo struggled to regain control of his emotions. His breath was forced, rasping, and she could feel and see the effort it cost him. He let go of her suddenly and Casey stumbled, almost dropping Mike's photo. She caught it before it reached the ground, but Ivo became aware of it for the first time and snatched it from her hands.

'No, give me that. It's mine.'

Casey tried to take it back, but Ivo held her off and moved under a light to see what it was. He recognised the photograph and turned to her in renewed fury. 'You're ex-boyfriend! Is he what this is all about? Was it because of him that you ran out on me?' He saw by her face that he was right, and in a fit of intense fury Ivo began to tear the photo into pieces.

'No! Don't!' She leapt at him and tried to get the photo from his hands, clawing and hitting out at him, then burst into tears as he threw the scraps violently out over the wall. 'You pig!'

She went to run past him to try to gather up the pieces, but Ivo caught her arm and swung her round. 'Does he mean so much to you still—this man you once trusted?' he demanded savagely.

'Yes,' Casey yelled back. 'He means everything to me.'

Ivo gave a snort of fury. 'And you're going to let some useless boyfriend who let you down and hurt you go on ruining your life?'

'He wasn't my boyfriend,' Casey retorted in bitter anguish. 'He was my husband!'

Ivo stared at her, her words making him freeze into stillness. 'What are you saying?' he demanded harshly, finding his voice.

'Mike was my husband. I loved him so much. And I can't stop loving him. That was why...I knocked his photo down when—when we were together and he came into my mind and I...' She gave á desolate sob. 'I felt that I was betraying him, being unfaithful to him.'

Letting go of her wrist, Ivo stepped back. 'Are you trying to tell me that you're still married to him?' he asked incredulously.

Slowly she shook her head. 'No.'

'You're divorced from him, then?'

Again she shook her head and moved over to the wall to look down at the sea where the scraps of Mike's photo clung to the waves. 'No. He. .' She tried to say it, but couldn't. 'He had a fatal illness.'

Ivo stared at her tensely; the silence between them suddenly filled with her sadness. He lifted a hand as if to put it on her shoulder in comfort, but then drew back. 'Why didn't you tell me?' he asked helplessly.

Her balled fists resting on the wall, Casey shook her head. 'I can't talk about it, even now. It was almost three years ago, but it seems like yesterday. The words are so hard, so final. And to say that you're a widow, especially when you're young; people look at you as if you're some kind of freak.' Her voice grew bitter. 'And men; they think there's only one way you want to be comforted. Even your friends' husbands. So I don't tell anyone and that way you don't get hurt and you don't get sympathy, because sympathy is worse than everything else.'

Ivo looked at her bent head, at her shoulders sagging under the load of her grief and, realising that she wouldn't want him to touch her, he sat down on the stone seat, but after a moment he said, 'Was your marriage a happy one, Casey?'

She lifted her head and nodded. 'Yes, very happy.'

'But you couldn't have been married for very long.'

'No, only four years.'

'And did your husband love you?'

Casey turned to stare at him. 'Of course he loved me.' She frowned. 'Why are you asking me these questions?'

'Because I think that if your husband loved you then he wouldn't want you to mourn for him for the rest of your life,' Ivo said urgently. 'He would want you to be happy. He would want you to find someone else and fall in love again.'

Casey lifted her head and looked up at the moonlit sky for a long moment before she said huskily, 'Yes, Mike would want that.'

Ivo got quickly to his feet and came towards her. 'Well, then...'

But she flinched away. 'No! I can't. You're just trying to find some means of persuading me to go to bed with you.'

His jawline hardening at her physical rejection, Ivo said harshly, 'And is that so terrible? I'm in love with you and I want you desperately. And I——'

'Are you—in love with me? You never said so before.'

'Oh, Casey.' He gave a rueful shake of his head. 'Surely you realised? Surely you must have seen how I felt about you every time I looked at you, touched you? I'm sure that everyone else in the team knows. Are you the only one who is so blind?' He gave a bitter laugh. 'Evidently you are. But tonight—I told you so often tonight, before...' He stopped, gritting his teeth.

'I'm sorry. I—I didn't hear. I was trying to close my mind to everything but—being with you.'

'But you didn't care about me,' Ivo said in sudden pain. 'Even though you were willing to go to bed with me. How could you have cared when you're still in love with someone else?'

'I did care,' Casey protested. '*I do care.* And I wanted to—to have you make love to me. I thought I could go through with it, and if Mike's photo hadn't fallen on the floor I would probably——'

'Are you trying to tell me that was an accident?' Ivo cut in. 'Of course it wasn't.'

'But I didn't do it on purpose. Why should I? I told you I wanted you too.'

'If you'd really cared about me, if you'd fallen in love with me, you'd have put that photo away, made it part of your past, not left it beside your bed where you only had to turn your head to see it while we were making love. OK, maybe you didn't consciously knock it down, but I'm willing to bet anything you like that something would have happened to make you stop.' He drew closer, looking into her face, and, his voice raw, said, 'You said you thought you could go through with it, as if having me make love to you was some sort of ordeal, so you must have had doubts and misgivings.'

She nodded slowly. 'I've never been with any other man than Mike. We met at art school and fell in love straight away. We got married when Mike and Steve started up Decart together. Everything was so wonderful, the company took off right from the start and the future was going to be so marvellous...' Her voice faltered but she went on, 'Then, afterwards, I didn't go out or see anyone for quite a while until Steve said I had to go and help him, that the company was falling apart. Work helped, it helped tremendously, and Steve made me a partner instead of Mike.'

'But you didn't go out with any other men?' Ivo probed.

'No.' She gave a vehement shake of her head. 'I didn't want to. Oh, a couple of times Steve's wife has asked me to dinner and there has been a man there that she invited along for me to meet, but it didn't work out. I—I couldn't feel anything. Except hate,' she added on a suddenly fierce note, 'when they tried to make a pass at me.'

'I saw Ray kissing you once,' Ivo reminded her.

'Did you?' She shrugged. 'It didn't mean anything. He was just trying me out and accepted it when I told him I wasn't interested.'

'And me?' Ivo asked shortly. 'Didn't my kisses mean anything either?'

She lowered her head for a moment and then looked at him candidly. 'Yes, they did. They meant—a great deal. That's why I was so afraid.'

'Afraid?'

She hesitated, not sure how to put her feelings into words. 'You turn me on,' she told him. 'I'm sorry if that sounds crude, but it's true. You make me go weak inside when you kiss me, and part of me—the physical part, I suppose—just longs for you to hold me and—and make love to me.'

She paused, her face flushed, and Ivo, his voice less sharp, said, 'And the other part of you?'

'That's the cowardly part. The part that has been hurt once so badly that it's terrified of being hurt again. And it's also the part that is still in love with Mike and made me feel guilty about being with you, as if I was betraying him in some way.' Turning her head to look at him, Casey said, 'I'm sorry, Ivo.'

'Are you? I doubt it,' he retorted on a harsh note. 'You've forgotten to say that you're also completely selfish.' She gave him a startled look and he went on, 'Did you bother to think of me when all this was going on in your head and your emotions? What was I, Casey, just some sort of laboratory specimen you were going to experiment on and then discard if it didn't work? Like now?'

'No! Of course not.' Casey gave him an appalled look. 'I told you; I liked you. You were the first man I'd felt anything for.'

'OK, so you liked me, and I turned you on, so you thought you'd let me persuade you into going to bed with me. But did it never once occur to you that I was falling hopelessly in love with you? That I'd waited all my life, and when I finally fell it was with a girl who was still in love with a dead man!'

Casey flinched at his last words, but there was such bitter anguish in his tone that she stared at him in stunned surprise. 'You never said that you loved me,' she said in distress. 'I thought—I thought that all you wanted was an affair. That's one of the reasons why I was afraid to let myself care about you too much. I thought that you might get tired of me and I would be so hurt, feel so cheap, and it would be—be an affront to Mike's memory.'

Ivo looked at her grimly at the mention of Mike's name, but he said, 'Are you saying that you stopped yourself from falling in love with me?'

She nodded reluctantly. 'Yes. Yes, I suppose so.'

'You said that was one of the reasons why you were afraid to fall in love with me; what was the other?'

A hunted expression came into Casey's eyes and she turned away. 'That was it, there wasn't anything else.'

'Don't lie to me, Casey.' Touching her for the first time since she'd told him about Mike, Ivo took hold of her shoulders and swung her round to face him. 'There was another reason, and I demand to know what it is.' He gave a bitter laugh. 'I think I have the right at least to know why you rejected me.'

She bit her lip and her eyes filled with tears again as she looked at him. 'I fought against falling for you,' she admitted. 'I tried very hard because—because I don't think I could bear to go through that again. If something happened to you . . . if you—if what happened to Mike happened to you . . .'

'If I died, you mean,' Ivo said deliberately. He gave a short laugh. 'Oh lord, Casey, who can tell what the future holds? All right, so you've been hurt once, terribly hurt, but is that any reason to deny yourself a second chance at happiness?' His grip tightened on her arm and he looked at her broodingly. 'I'm beginning to think that that's why you shut your eyes to the way I felt about you; you convinced yourself that all I wanted was an affair, or even just a holiday romance, and that helped you not to fall in love with me.'

She shook her head. 'Maybe it should have done, but it didn't.'

His voice sharpened. 'What do you mean?'

'I tried not to fall in love with you—but I didn't succeed. When you went away I missed you dreadfully, and when you came back tonight—when I saw you, I knew then that I was in love with you. I think I had been all along but I wouldn't let myself believe it. Can you possibly think I would have been willing to go to bed with you unless I really cared?'

He stared at her. 'But if you love me . . .'

'But the guilt is still there. And so is the love for Mike. I can't shut him out, Ivo. I tried and I can't.'

Slowly, almost tentatively, Ivo drew her into his arms. She trembled, but he stroked her back gently as he said, 'Maybe you shouldn't try. He will always be an important part of your life, so let him have that part. And we will have the future.'

But Casey shook her head and stepped away from him. 'What future could we possibly have after tonight?'

'If we love each other enough, we'll make a future for ourselves,' Ivo said resolutely.

Casey looked up at him, his features hardened into determination by the moonlight, and almost felt that she could believe him. She would have liked to believe him, but she sighed and said, 'It wouldn't work. Every time we went to bed together you'd be suspicious that I was thinking of Mike, and every time you had a headache or a pain I'd be terrified that you were going to get ill.'

Putting his hand under her chin, Ivo said, 'Do you think me so little of a man that I couldn't make you think of me and no one but me when I make love to you?' She caught her breath, remembering the expertise of his lovemaking and how much she'd wanted him. 'And although I couldn't guarantee not to get run down by a bus,' he went on, deliberately keeping his voice light, 'I will guarantee to go on loving you for as long as I live.'

She gazed into his eyes for such a long moment that Ivo began to hope that he had won her round, but then Casey blinked and, stepping away from him, said in a voice of such shocking bitterness that it frightened him, 'And can you guarantee that you won't ever get cancer, and that I won't have to watch you slowly die, day by day, in ever greater pain, for more than a year? Well, can you?'

Ivo sat down on the stone bench and put his face in his hands. 'Why the hell didn't you tell me?'

'How could I? I wasn't sure how you felt, and even if I had been it wouldn't have been fair to lay all that on you.'

He looked up. 'So just what did you intend when you went to bed with me tonight, Casey?'

Her face suddenly intense, she said, 'I wanted to forget everything but my own body—and yours. To cut out the past and be just the two of us until it was time to go home. To be free to love you and give you what you wanted, because I knew that you wanted me very much.' Her voice softened. 'And I needed you, so desperately. I yearned to be held and loved again. But it had to be by you. I didn't want anyone else but you.'

'Oh, my poor darling.' Ivo caught her hand and carried it to his lips. But then his brows drew into a frown. 'But you said until it was time to go home?'

'Yes.' She nodded. 'It would have been for just these two days. I'd made up my mind that when I got back to England I would never see you again. That way I wouldn't get hurt, and—and I would have given you what you wanted.'

Ivo's face tightened and he drew himself up. 'I see. And do you really think I would have been satisfied with that? That I would have just let you go?'

'I would have made you happy. Given you . . .' She turned to him and saw the pain in his face and the words died on her lips. 'No, not now.'

'No.' He raised an unsteady hand to push his hair off his forehead. 'Hell, you're a coward, Casey. Don't you realise that you would have been running away again? Oh, all right, I know that you think you have cause enough, but couldn't you have found the courage to follow your own heart, to risk whatever might happen in the future? Isn't the chance of love worth that much?' She was silent, and he suddenly rounded on her and took hold of her arms. 'Then I'll just have to be brave enough for both of us. Because I'm not going to let you go, Casey. It's taken me a hell of a long time to find you, and I love you and I'm going to marry you. And we're going to live as long and as happily as we can. Do you understand?' He gave her a shake. 'Well? Do you?'

'Yes. Yes, but——'

'No buts,' he ordered. 'You can consider yourself engaged. And there'll be no more secrets, Casey. In future we share everything. You can tell me all about Mike, and maybe I'll tell you about one or two of my girlfriends. OK?'

Casey gave a small smile, but shook her head. 'That wouldn't be fair to you. I don't know that I can ever forget Mike enough to——'

'Don't try,' he interrupted her. 'If you make a conscious effort to forget him, it will only bring him into your mind more.' Putting his hands on either side of her face, he said earnestly, 'But I want you to promise that you'll think of me and the way you feel about me. Will you do that?'

Looking up into his eyes, Casey smiled. 'It would be very difficult not to think about you,' she admitted.

'Good. Then I'll just have to make sure that you think about nothing else,' he said softly, and bent to kiss her.

For a moment she resisted him, her body stiffening, but then she made a conscious effort to relax, although her hands were balled into fists at her sides.

'There, that wasn't so hard, was it?' Ivo asked as he raised his head.

'No.' In a sudden burst of honesty, she said, 'Having you kiss me and hold me is the easiest thing in the world. If that was all you wanted from me I could . . .' Her voice trailed off as she saw his face harden. 'But that wouldn't be enough, would it?'

'Of course not,' he answered brusquely. 'I'm as human as the next man, Casey. I want you in every sense, for your sake as well as mine. Because we'll never be truly happy until you commit yourself to me, willingly and completely.' He paused, looking down into her face, and then sighed. 'But I'm willing to give you some time, if that's what you want. I won't——' his mouth twisted wryly, 'I won't force myself on you. But you've got to make up your mind what it is you want, Casey: to go on living in the past or to find the courage to go forward and find happiness in the future. I won't go on waiting indefinitely. That would be too hard to bear.'

She nodded. 'Yes, I can understand that. Thank you.'

Ivo gave a short, grim laugh. 'Don't thank me yet; I've an idea I'm going to find the next few weeks very difficult to get through.' He saw her shiver and put his arm round her. 'You're getting cold. Come on, let's go back.'

As they walked through the village the first faint glow of dawn began to appear in the sky, breaking over the houses and the distant hills that were the beginning of the Fire Mountains. They walked as quietly as they could through the still sleeping complex, and found the door of her bungalow standing wide as Ivo had left it when he had come after her. They went inside, but the broken glass was still over the floor.

'You can't stay here,' Ivo said definitely. 'Collect a few clothes and come back to my bungalow for what's left of the night.'

Casey half opened her mouth to protest, but saw the firmness in his face and said instead, 'Yes, all right.'

There was enough light when they reached Ivo's place for them not to bother to switch on the light. Ivo walked straight into the bedroom and said, 'I've been sleeping in the bed on the left, so you can have the other.' He turned and raised a quizzical eyebrow. 'Unless you'd like to sleep with me, of course—and I do mean sleep.'

'Thanks, but—I think I'd better take this one.' And Casey touched the right-hand bed.

'OK.' He disappeared into the bathroom and came out a few minutes later wearing just the bottom half of a pair of pyjamas. 'The bathroom's all yours.' And he got into bed.

It took Casey a little while to clean the dried blood from her hands and knees. When she went back into the bedroom Ivo appeared to be asleep and she crept across the room, afraid of waking him. She slid into the bed and pulled the cover over her, feeling suddenly deathly tired as soon as her head touched the pillow. But sleep wouldn't come. She lay gazing at the ceiling, thinking unhappily over the past few hours and wondering what the future held in store. If Ivo had his way, everything would be simple and clear-cut, but when was life ever simple? Casey had found that out the hard way, additionally so tonight. She wanted to please him, to give him what he so desperately wanted, but she realised that she was in love with both men, the living and the dead. And Ivo had said he wouldn't settle for less than total commitment. Oh, he would let her keep her memories, but he would expect her to bury them deep in her heart and... Bury them as she had buried Mike, she thought bitterly. A small sob broke from her and she quickly tried to stifle it.

'Stop thinking about it.' Ivo's harsh voice grated through the silent room. 'Worrying isn't going to help. Here, give me your hand.' He reached out across the gap and Casey reluctantly put her hand into his. He kissed her fingers and said, 'Now go to sleep. Everything will seem better in the morning.'

She let her hand rest in his, but later, when she'd decided from his breathing that he must have gone to sleep, Casey eased her hand away. She lay still for a while, staring up at the gradually lightening ceiling, then slipped out of bed and went to stand at the window, a slender, pale figure, gazing up at the distant hills that were turned to fire again in the brilliant pink light of the dawn.

Ivo had opened his eyes the moment she moved, but he lay still, watching her with a grim look on his face and the now familiar ache for her burning his soul. His face changed, became bleak as he saw her unhappiness, and he, too, wondered what the future held for them. But the bleakness hardened into resolve as he determined to do everything within his power to bring them together—whether Casey liked it or not.

CHAPTER EIGHT

THEY flew back to England early on Monday morning. Casey sat next to Ivo, but there was an air of strain between them that they were able to hide from everyone else but not from themselves. It showed in small things, the tightness of Ivo's mouth and the smudged circles of tiredness around Casey's eyes. Any of the others who noticed the latter put her tiredness down to completely different reasons, of course. But they couldn't have been more wrong.

On Sunday morning, after their sleepless night, Ivo had said firmly that they were going to spend the day lazing in the sun, and they had taken a couple of loungers out by the pool soon after breakfast. Others in the team had gradually wandered out to join them, most of them suffering from some degree of hangover. Only Lucy seemed to be full of energy that morning, and she kept worrying at Ivo until he agreed to go and play a set of tennis with her before it got too hot. Casey watched them go, Lucy in just a bikini and tennis shoes, and Ivo in a pair of shorts, his skin tanned to a deep brown by the sun. He had a beautiful physique, she thought. Just looking at him made her aware of him. She remembered him last night, standing over her, and how much she had wanted him, hungered for him. And yet it had all gone so hopelessly wrong.

Ivo had said that her knocking Mike's photo down had been psychological, if it hadn't been that she would have found something else to stop her giving herself to him. And maybe he was right. The very idea that she was incapable of physically loving another man troubled Casey deeply, but the sense of guilt was still very strong. She tried to drown it, to tell herself that Mike would have wanted her to be happy, but her mind was full of doubt and anxiety.

Seeing the make-up girl looking round for someone to talk to, Casey closed her eyes and pretended to be asleep; the last thing she wanted right now was someone prying, and the girl had become renowned for her nosiness since they had been on Lanzarote. Her thoughts went back to other summers when she had been married to Mike, before he had become ill. They had gone abroad for the sun always, and usually to an apartment near quiet beaches or some scenic place where they would spend contented hours sketching together. But Mike had been, like many artistic men, an earthy and enthusiastic lover, wanting to take her whenever he felt the need. He had greatly enjoyed sex and given her enjoyment too, from his vigour and enthusiasm, but he had been a selfish lover in that he had mostly taken it for granted that she would enjoy it and had done little to make sure that she did.

Not like Ivo. He was far more experienced and knew exactly how to arouse her to the heights of excitement. Casey had found that out, if nothing else, last night. She wondered how many women he had had to become so sure, so skilful in his knowledge of a woman's body. It occurred to her that she ought to feel jealous of these other women, but she didn't. Did that mean she wasn't in love with Ivo, that she had been fooling herself? Was that why she had been unable to go through with it? The tortured thoughts filled her brain, giving her no peace and no solutions. She felt angry and resentful, almost wishing that she had never met Ivo. She was afraid that he would want her to go to bed with him again tonight, even though he had said he would give her some time, and she was terrified of what might happen.

The fear of another failure made her prickly and antagonistic for the rest of the day. She answered Ivo shortly when he came back, and after giving her a sharp glance he lowered himself into his lounger and calmly went to sleep, which only annoyed her more. He woke up at about twelve and they swam and then ate lunch with some of the others out on the terrace below the bar. Ray Brent was all over one of the model girls, a romance that seemed to have blossomed since last night, and no one was surprised when the two of them disappeared into Ray's bungalow soon after lunch.

Ten pairs of eyes watched them go, and Ivo said drily, 'He seems to have got over your rejection of him remarkably quickly.'

'There's been time enough. And besides,' Casey added tartly, 'it was only a try-on. He just went for the most advantageous bet first.'

Ivo turned to look at her and raised an eyebrow. 'Meaning?'

'That I often have to hire models and so I'm in a position to give quite regular work to anyone I particularly favour,' Casey answered baldly.

'And do you really believe that was the case?'

She shrugged. 'What else? It's what people would have thought if I'd been receptive.' She paused, then added heavily, 'And exactly what they must think of you and I now—that I'm going with you solely because of what I can get out of you. After all, you are in a position to put a lot of work my way and——'

'Shut up!' Ivo said forcefully, pushing himself upright and swinging his legs to the ground. There was a flash of anger in his eyes as he said, 'Anyone with half an eye can see that isn't true.' He gave a grim smile and added with wry emphasis, 'And *you* certainly know it isn't, so why try and cheapen what we have by suggesting it?'

Casey's cheeks reddened. 'I'm—I'm sorry,' she muttered, and lifted a hand to shield her face.

But Ivo leant forward and pulled her hand down, then gently began to stroke it. 'I think that right now you're wishing me in hell, aren't you?' he said unexpectedly. 'Well, I can understand that. All your emotions are completely mixed up, your values overturned, and you're blaming me for making you face up to things when it would be a hell of a lot easier to run away and hide. But I've a feeling you've been hiding for too long, Casey, and if you don't face up to the fact that you've got to start living and feeling again right now, then you never will.' Casey turned to listen to him and her eyes grew wide and pleading, but he shook his head and said, 'But I'm not going to ease up on you or start feeling sorry for you, my darling, because I love you and want you too much.' He smiled. 'Don't worry, we'll sort it out.'

Getting to his feet, he drew her up beside him. 'Come on, let's go and hire a boat.'

But Casey remembered the last time they had been on a boat together, and decided she couldn't take being alone and so close to him, so she shook her head.

'No, why don't we just walk down to the beach and have a drink in one of the bars there?'

'All right.'

Although he agreed readily enough, Casey was fully aware that Ivo knew all her reasons. He knows too much, she thought on a spurt of anger, but was immediately ashamed; she ought to be grateful that he understood her feelings. She only wished she understood them herself.

Somehow she got through the rest of the day, the only relief coming when she went over to her own bungalow to change for dinner. The maid had been in and all the broken glass was gone; there was only the empty frame left tidily on the chest of drawers. Casey picked it up, not really needing the photograph to see Mike's face smiling at her, so well did she remember it. But it had been a part of her life since the day he'd died, on her bedside-table at home and on her desk in the office, and going with her every time she went away. And she had the negative at home, she could quite easily get another print. That thought comforted her at first, until she remembered Ivo's anger and his forceful declaration that if she'd really loved him she would have put the photograph away. But it had never even occurred to her to do so. So what did that mean? Oh, damn him! she thought resentfully, and pushed the frame into the drawer.

Last night had been the hair-down celebration, tonight was the formal farewell when everyone had decided to dress up. So Casey changed into a black-lace dress and put her hair up into a formal style that made her look sophisticated, but also gave her an air of fragile beauty, although her face was taut, her mouth moody.

She took her time and was only just ready when
Ivo came to call for her. The front door was unlocked
and he walked casually into the sitting-room, as if he
had the right. But maybe he did. He called out to let
her know he was there, and after a few minutes Casey
walked to the door of the bedroom and into the sitting-
room. Ivo was wearing his white dinner-jacket again,
which looked even better now that his skin was so
tanned. He swung round when he heard her come into
the room, a greeting on his lips. But the words died
as he stared at her, his eyes widening into a look of
intense love and longing. Then he let out his breath
on a harsh sigh. 'You look very lovely, so beautiful.
Every time I see you I fall deeper in love with you.'
He came to her and went to kiss her, but she turned
her head at the last moment and he only kissed her
cheek. His mouth twisted wryly. 'But you're not in
the mood for that, are you?'

But he was wrong; his words and his look had
caught at her heart so that she felt torn in two again,
and it was that she couldn't bear. She raised her head
to tell him so, but saw the smouldering anger in his
eyes, and instead said huskily, 'Let's go to dinner.'

Surprisingly, Casey enjoyed that meal, the last with
all the team together. On the whole the shoot had gone
very well, there had been few disagreements, and the
only nastiness had been when they had got Lucy
drunk. But they were a well-knit team now, with Lucy
a full part of it, and Casey was more than pleased
with the photographs that Chas had taken. Once she
had incorporated them into the page designs, with
Vulcan's name discreetly added to each one, she knew
that they would have a winner on their hands, a great

advert for Vulcan and a sure work-producer for Decart as well.

At the end of the meal, as they were all exchanging telephone numbers and making promises to keep in touch and let the others know of any work going, Pedro, the restaurant owner, who had become a friend during the past weeks, came over with small gifts for each of them—embroidered handkerchiefs for the ladies and bottles of wine for the men. And for Casey there was a special present, a beautifully embroidered tablecloth with four matching napkins. 'Because you will soon be a señora not a señorita, no?' Pedro told her with a roguish look at Ivo.

Casey didn't know what to say, she could only thank him for his kindness and promise to eat there again every time she came to the island. Ivo, of course, thought it was hugely amusing and only grinned at her embarrassment, but then he winked at her and she was able to laugh and smile back.

It was late when they all finally left the restaurant, the last to leave. Someone suggested going down to the bar again, but after last night no one had enough energy and they all made their slow way back to the complex to pack before going to bed. Casey's nerves increased the nearer they got, and she tensed when Ivo put a familiar arm round her waist.

'Did you do any packing before dinner?' he asked.

'No. Did you?'

'You forget; I don't have much to pack.' There was gentle irony in his tone at this reminder that he had flown all the way back here just to see her. Or rather, to go to bed with her. Casey's heart hardened a little until she remembered that she had asked him to try to come back; and if that wasn't a promise of a good time to come she didn't know what was.

They said goodnight to the others and strolled over to her bungalow, but before they reached it Casey stopped and raised her head to look at him. Ivo's face was withdrawn, his shoulders involuntarily braced as he waited for her to speak, expecting another rebuff. But his brows flickered as she said, 'I've been very unfair to you, haven't I? You were fully entitled to expect me to fall into your arms after all the encouragement I gave you. Especially as you came all the way back here just so that we could—could be together. You must have been very disappointed and I'm—I'm very sorry.'

'Disappointed is rather an understatement.' But Ivo's voice was mild. Putting his hand on her arm, he drew her towards him and kissed her gently on the mouth. 'But thanks for the apology.' His hand tightened a little and he kissed her again, but felt her stiffen and so drew back. He looked at her, his eyes hooded, then said in sudden urgency, 'Casey, I want very much to go to bed with you. Not to make love, just to hold you, to sleep with you and be there when you wake. I think that that way we'll conquer these guilt feelings you have and——'

'No!' She gave him an amazed look. 'You know that wouldn't work. How could we possibly spend the night together without you wanting to make love? You said yourself how desperately you wanted me. And you said you'd give me time,' she reminded him, her voice rising to a slightly hysterical note.

'Don't you think I can control myself?' Ivo demanded, becoming angry.

'No, I don't think you could,' Casey declared roundly.

'Well, thanks for the vote of confidence. Your previous experience has clearly given you a very poor opinion of men's powers of control,' he snapped. He glared at her a moment, then shoved his hands in his pockets. 'I'm sorry, I had no right to say that. Maybe it wasn't such a good idea, after all,' he admitted moodily. 'You obviously don't trust me.'

'No,' Casey said after a moment, 'I'm the one who should apologise—again. You kept your word last night and I have no real reason to think that you wouldn't tonight. But I just can't—I don't think I'd be able to sleep,' she amended hastily. 'I'm sorry.'

'But you still haven't said that you trust me,' Ivo pointed out.

'It isn't a question of trust.'

He gave her a derisive look. 'No? What, then?'

Raising her head, Casey looked up at the stars glinting in the thick blackness of the sky. 'It's a question of fear, and guilt. My fear, my guilt, and I have to try and fight them—alone.'

'You don't have to be alone, Casey.'

'No, I know that,' she acknowledged in a softer tone. 'But being close to you only makes it worse. I feel—under pressure from you. Can you understand that?'

'Yes, I think so,' he said heavily. 'But I'm not going to just walk away, Casey, so don't think it.'

'All right, but I need time—and I need space.' She paused, but he didn't say anything, so she looked at him pleadingly. 'Will you give me that?'

He made an impatient, angry gesture. 'You've got it all wrong. What you need is love and closeness.

You need to learn that you can trust me—in every way. And you must trust in your own feelings and needs. You must trust life itself. Cutting yourself off from me isn't going to help; you'll just build that wall round yourself again, but doubly thick this time. Darling, you must be brave,' he said intensely. 'And you have to find it within yourself. I can't give it to you, as much as I want to.'

Casey shook her head wretchedly. 'I'm sorry, I can't do what you want. Not now. Not yet.'

With a fed-up sigh, Ivo put his hand on her shoulder. 'All right, I won't force you—although I have an idea that everything would be fine if I did,' he muttered under his breath. 'Goodnight, then, my love. I'll see you tomorrow.' He kissed her again in brief urgency, then turned and strode briskly away.

When they landed in London, Casey found that Steve had come to meet her with the company Range Rover as they had to take all the costumes and put them into store, just in case anything went wrong and some of the shots had to be taken again. So it was both awkward and yet a relief to have to say goodbye to Ivo at the airport. He insisted on kissing her, much to Steve's surprise, and told her he would phone her that evening, then went off with Lucy to collect his own car.

Steve was bursting with curiosity, but Casey fielded all his questions and insisted on talking about work until he got the message. They went straight back to the office and Casey worked late, catching up on all that had been happening while she'd been in Lanzarote. Like every first day back at work, it soon felt as if she'd never been away as she slipped back into her old routine. Her nice, safe routine of long and hard work that she'd built as a protection against loneliness and grief. And which was rudely shattered at about seven-thirty when Ivo rang.

'I thought you'd have left by now,' he remarked. 'I've been trying to phone you at home.'

'There's been a lot to catch up on.'

'I'll come and pick you up, and we'll have dinner.'

'Oh, but . . .' Casey started to protest, but recognised the determination in his tone. 'I haven't had time to change.'

'All right, I'll drive you to your place first and we'll go on from there. See you in about twenty minutes.'

He rang off, giving Casey no time to argue. She finished what she was doing, then carried her cases down to the foyer of the building and waited for him there. It was raining, not very hard but enough to make passers-by put up their umbrellas. Pulling open the door, Casey stepped out on to the pavement and breathed in the familiar scents of the city, heightened by the rain. A car swung out of the traffic into the kerb and Ivo got out. He looked at her quizzically. 'Enjoying the rain?'

She nodded and smiled. 'I didn't realise how much I'd missed it. Lanzarote was so hot, and the rain there was more of a torrential downpour, but this is the gentle rain from heaven.'

'And just as merciful.' Taking her in his arms, Ivo kissed her right there, out in the rain, then smiled at her. 'I love you,' he said softly. He kissed her again, holding her close, and she felt his body begin to harden before he quickly let her go. He grinned unashamedly at her surprised look. 'One day I'm going to make love to you in the rain,' he promised, then turned and picked up her cases. 'Come on, we'll get soaked.'

It didn't take long to reach Casey's flat in the car, but her cousin, Tina, was still staying there and had to be introduced to Ivo. Casey left them talking together while she changed, and tried to ignore the look of approving shrewdness that Tina gave her as they left.

But she might have known her cousin wouldn't let it alone. Tina was waiting up to talk to her when she came in around midnight and said, 'Well, aren't you the sly one? Where have you been hiding him? He's gorgeous.'

'If you mean Ivo Maine, then I've only recently met him. He's a business associate, that's all,' Casey said dismissively.

'Well, that might be all he is at the moment, but not for long,' Tina observed. 'Why, anyone can see that he's crazy about you.' She sighed. 'I just wish I could meet someone like him.'

'Why, when you already have a husband who loves you?'

As she'd hoped, this led Tina into a repeat performance of all her problems to which Casey only half listened, but her ears pricked when Tina said, 'And now Brian's found out that I'm staying here and he's forever phoning and coming round.' She said it grumblingly, but there was a note of complacency there too.

She's deliberately giving him the run-around, Casey thought, and hardened her attitude towards her cousin. 'I hope you've found somewhere to live,' she said tersely.

Tina, five years older and darker in colouring than Casey, looked at her in surprise. 'I thought I'd live here with you.'

'Well, you thought wrong. I don't want to share the flat,' she said firmly, determining not to let Tina take her hospitality for granted.

She got an indignant look in return, but then Tina grinned and said, 'Oh, I see. You want to—er—entertain your boyfriend here. Well, I can't say I blame you. But you don't have to worry about me, you know; I can go into my room or I can even go out if you'll just let me know in advance when you want to bring him.'

'That is not what I want,' Casey declared in annoyance. Deciding to be hard, she said, 'Look, Tina, you've left Brian, right? Well, don't expect to dump yourself permanently on me, because I don't want you. It was your decision and now you have to start to make a new life for yourself—on your own. Just as I had to. You've got to go out and get yourself a job and earn your own living, not let Brian go on paying all your bills.'

'My financial arrangements are nothing to do with you,' Tina declared, taking an aloof tone.

'Yes, they are, because you're living rent-free in my flat. And because you've been bending my ear with all your so-called problems for the last couple of weeks. If you don't want me to have anything to do with it, then you shouldn't have told me.'

'I expected your help and encouragement, not this.'

'And that's what you're getting,' Casey retorted. 'You've been dependent on someone all your life. First your parents, and then Brian and now me. You have no children to teach you responsibility, so you just cling. Well, maybe you aren't in love with Brian any more, but don't expect me to stand in for him. You have two choices, Tina: you either go back to Brian, or try to make it on your own. But you have to do one of them and do it fast.'

Tina gave her an angry, affronted look. 'I should have thought you'd have been glad of my company. I could have gone to stay with several of my friends, but I knew you were on your own, working till all hours because you're so lonely, and never going out. That's why I came here. I thought I was doing you a favour.'

'Well, you're not,' Casey returned shortly. 'Or yourself.'

'All right, I'll find somewhere else and go. Unless you'd like me to leave tonight, of course,' Tina added sarcastically.

'On the phone you said you only wanted some-where to stay for a few days—that was nearly two weeks ago,' Casey reminded her. And, satisfied that she'd made her point, added, 'I'm not throwing you out. Just find somewhere and start living your own life, that's all.' She put a weary hand up to her head. 'I'm tired, I'm going to bed. Goodnight.'

Tina gave her a grumpy goodnight and added in a mutter loud enough for Casey to hear, 'All this just because she wants to bring her lovers here. I wonder how many she's had since Mike died. And her letting everyone believe she's a grieving widow.'

The next couple of weeks were very difficult ones for Casey. She tried to avoid Ivo but he wouldn't let her, seeing her as often as he could and always phoning her every day when they couldn't meet. He was as patient with her as he knew how, but his need, his aching yearning for her, grew every time he saw her. And as he saw no reason to hide it she was under constant pressure to give him what he wanted so badly. The tension between them became electric, taut with frustration, and so strong that other people noticed it.

Casey tried to behave normally, but she was so worried and mixed up that her work began to suffer. Steve was very good about it, especially as she couldn't bring herself to confide in him, but even he began to get impatient when she completely forgot an important meeting and he had to try to placate a potential client. The only good thing was that Tina had moved out and gone to stay with friends, but had evidently neglected to tell her husband, because Brian came round to the flat a couple of evenings later looking for her. He had had a few drinks to give him courage, and was most upset when Tina wasn't there. He insisted on staying to pour his side of the story into Casey's unwilling ears, and seemed genuinely puzzled that Tina had left him as he had been perfectly happy.

'I'm sure there must be some man she hasn't told me about,' he declared angrily, unable to believe that Tina could have got bored with him. 'I'll kill him if there is.'

Realising that he was the type who wasn't used to drinking and got belligerent when he did, Casey managed to persuade him to go home, and thought herself lucky to be no longer involved. So she was far from pleased when she came home from work and found Tina back at the flat.

'What are you doing here?' she demanded. 'And how did you get in?'

'Now, don't get angry,' Tina said placatingly. 'The friends I went to are having guests to stay and there isn't enough room for me, so I'll only be here for a few days.'

'You haven't said how you got in.'

'Oh, well, actually I had a spare key cut while I was here. Just in case I lost the other, you know. I'm always losing keys.'

Biting back her anger, Casey said, 'Do you know that Brian came here looking for you?'

'Yes, he keeps on at me to go back to him,' Tina answered smugly.

'So why don't you?'

'No, that would be too much of a victory for him. He's got to be shaken out of his apathy first. I'm not going to make it easy for him.'

Casey looked at her cousin in exasperation. 'What are you doing? Testing his love for you or something? I don't think you've any real intention of leaving him at all,' she said disgustedly, adding, 'You're a fool, Tina. You ought to be damn glad that you've got him. And you're playing with fire. Brian loves you and you're driving him mad all for nothing. He'd been drinking and he was almost distracted when he came here the other night. Either break with him completely or go back to him. It isn't fair to play around with his love for you like this.'

'Oh, really?' Tina bristled. 'And what about you and Ivo? I'm not blind, you know. It's obvious that he's crazy about you and yet you keep *him* dangling.'

Casey flushed. 'You know nothing about it.' She turned and went into her own room to get ready to go out to dinner with Ivo, angry that Tina should equate her and Ivo's situation with her own. It isn't like that, she thought, I'm not deliberately keeping him dangling.

But nevertheless she was rather silent and thoughtful that evening. They went to the theatre, but she couldn't concentrate on the play, going over Tina's remark in her mind, blurted out in anger admittedly but possibly no less true because of that. She moved restlessly in her seat and Ivo gave her a swift, troubled look, wondering what was on her mind. Taking hold of her hand, he squeezed it reassuringly and watched for her reaction. She gave him back only a tentative smile, but left her hand in his till the end of the performance.

'Would you like to go and have supper somewhere?' he asked when they left the theatre. 'Or we can go and have a drink at a club, if you'd rather.'

'I would like a drink,' Casey replied, but added hesitantly, 'But I don't really feel like going to a nightclub. Couldn't we go—go somewhere quieter?'

'To your place, do you mean?' Ivo asked, trying to keep his voice level.

She shook her head. 'Tina has moved back with me.'

'I see. How about my place, then?'

She took a deep breath. 'Yes, I—yes, OK.'

Casey hadn't been to Ivo's flat before. It was in the Barbican, in one of several modern blocks built around the huge theatre and leisure complex, with water gardens and a plaza, that had been one of the first to be built in central London. The flat wasn't huge, but it was certainly luxurious in a very masculine way. As Ivo took her coat, Casey looked round and couldn't help wondering how many other women he'd brought here. She felt suddenly shy and tried to brazen it out. 'Some pad you've got here,' she remarked flippantly. 'I suppose you've got built-in everything. Drinks cabinet, stereo, wardrobes, television. Is there anything you haven't got, Ivo?' she demanded, a sardonic note in her voice.

He turned from the drinks cabinet to look at her. 'I haven't got the one thing I most want in the world,' he replied evenly. 'I haven't got a wife. I haven't got you.'

Immediately she felt ashamed. She took the drink he held out to her and lowered her head, but her hair was up and she couldn't hide behind its silken curtain.

'What did you think of the play?' Ivo asked, crossing to a leather chesterfield and sitting down, his legs crossed.

She looked down broodingly at her drink for a long moment, then said, 'I'm afraid I didn't concentrate on it very much. I was thinking of something else, something that Tina said to me tonight.'

'Oh, what was that?'

I told her to either leave her husband or go back to him, not to leave him dangling in mid-air. And she told me that that was exactly what I was doing to you.'

'I see.' Ivo raised his glass to his lips, only the whiteness of his knuckles betraying his inner tension.

'And I see now that she's right. That's very unfair of me, isn't it?' Casey went on. 'I—I have to make up my mind what I'm going to do.'

Ivo put down the glass and stood up, his face suddenly drawn. 'There's only one way I'm going to let you make up your mind,' he said on a harsh note of certainty. 'Millions of other people have been widowed and found happiness with someone else. You're not unique, Casey.' Then, being deliberately cruel, he said forcefully, 'I'm not going to let a dead man come between us.'

Casey flinched and looked up into his face, her eyes wide and vulnerable. 'Yes, I know. That—that's why I asked you to bring me here. Because I realised that there's only one way we're ever going to find out if it was psychological or——'

Her words were cut off as Ivo swept her into his arms and kissed her with a hunger that had too long been held in check. Passion gripped him from the first moment and he gave her no time to change her mind, covering her face with kisses, his hands caressing her and fumbling with her clothes all at the same time. Too eager and impatient to wait, he picked her up in his arms and carried her over to the bedroom, shouldering open the door and laying her down on the big double bed.

An oath of fury, terrible in its frustration and anguish, rent the silence of the lamp-lit room as Ivo rolled on to his back and lay gazing up at the ceiling, his hands balled into tight fists as he strove to control himself, his lips drawn back into a snarl of bitterness and raw pain.

'I'm sorry. I'm so sorry.' Casey scrambled off the bed and pulled on her clothes as quickly as she could. Little sobs of despair caught in her breath and she kept giving Ivo swift looks of fear and guilt. But he didn't move or speak, just lay there rigidly.

Casey felt that she could have borne it better if he had raged at her, as he had every right to do. But his silence frightened her more than any outburst of fury, and this put her on the defensive. She pushed her feet into her shoes and then ran for the door, but when she reached it she glanced back and saw that Ivo had turned his head to look at her, his dark eyes malevolent in his set face.

'Don't look at me like that,' she yelled at him. 'It's your own fault. You wouldn't let me alone. You pressurised me until I was so afraid of failure that it—it became inevitable.' Ivo didn't answer, just lay there looking at her with that dark, bleak look in his eyes until Casey gave a sob and ran out of the flat, slamming the door behind her.

After that fiasco Ivo made no attempt to contact Casey, and she didn't see him for another two weeks when she was forced to contact him to get his final approval for the calendar shots. She made an appointment with Marilyn, his secretary, and turned up at his office on a bright sunny morning. But their meeting was anything but bright and sunny. Ivo was polite, distant, very businesslike, and so cold that Casey shivered. She glanced once at his glacier-grey eyes and took care not to meet them again. She went through the calendar pages and printing arrangements as quickly as possible, so that less than an hour later she was back out in the street and wishing that her frozen senses could thaw in the heat.

She went home from work that evening still feeling numb and terribly alone. For once she would have welcomed her cousin's company, but Tina had left two days before to stay with her friends again so Casey was left with her own thoughts and a dreadful sense of emptiness. She had lost Ivo, she knew that now. Any frail, lingering hope had been completely dashed

by his behaviour today. And it was all her own fault.
Because she hadn't been able to shut Mike's memory
away into some private compartment of her heart and
mind, she had lost the chance of happiness with
another man. Well, she would just have to live with
that, as she had learnt to live without Mike. But now,
in the loneliness of the night, Casey found this second
loss almost harder to bear.

It was nearly eleven when Casey's doorbell rang a
couple of nights later. She was just changing to go to
bed but, with the wild hope that it might be Ivo
surging through her veins, she pulled on a robe and
went to answer the door. It wasn't Ivo, of course. It
was Brian, demanding to speak to Tina.

'She isn't here,' Casey told him. 'She left a few days
ago.'

'I don't believe you. She just told you to say that.'
Brian pushed open the door and strode into the flat
belligerently. 'Tina!' He yelled out his wife's name
and went into every room, even looking into the
wardrobe.

Casey waited impatiently by the door for him to
go, but Brian had been drinking again and grabbed
hold of her arm. 'Where is she?' he demanded. 'She's
gone to some man, hasn't she? I've had enough, d'you
understand? I've taken about as much as I can stand
from that bitch!'

'Well, she isn't here,' Casey told him shortly.
'You've seen that for yourself. Why don't you leave
it until tomorrow and then ring round some of her
friends? I don't know where she's staying.'

'Yes, you do. You must know.' Brian began to shake
her, beads of sweat standing out on his forehead. 'Tell

me where she is, damn you. I want her, do you hear? I want my wife!'

'Let go of me. If I knew where she was, I'd tell you. I'm as fed up with this affair as you are. I don't— Oh!'

Casey's words ended in a gasp of horror as Brian suddenly pulled open her robe and then began to run his hands over her and try to kiss her. His breath was revolting. Casey jerked her head away, retching, and began to remonstrate with him, but found herself fighting him off in earnest as he tore at her night-dress. But Brian was big and drunk and driven beyond the limits of endurance. She screamed, and he cursed and hit her. Casey staggered back against the hall-table, picked up the vase off it and threw it at him. It caught Brian on the shoulder, then crashed on to the floor. He gave a snarl of anger and came after her, arms outstretched. Casey fled back into the flat and locked herself in the bathroom.

Brian beat on the door with his fists, shouting and yelling, then the door shook as something heavy crashed against it. Other crashing sounds followed. Terrified, Casey pushed open the window and leaned out, screaming for help at the top of her voice.

It came quickly enough. Her neighbour called the police and then came round with them himself, armed with a golf club. When they burst through the door and Brian saw them, he collapsed into tears, looking around him in a dazed way as if he didn't know where he was or what he'd done. And when Casey came out of the bathroom, still quivering with fright and saw that in his fury he had completely wrecked her flat, she stood in stunned, appalled dismay.

'Will you be pressing charges, miss?' the policeman asked her when they had taken Brian away to sleep it off.

'No. His—his wife left him. He couldn't help it, he's not used to drinking.'

'Well, you'd better make *her* pay for all this damage, then,' the man said tersely, and left Casey alone amid the chaos.

She sank to the floor in the middle of the room among the broken furniture and shattered belongings. All the precious things that Mike had given her or they had bought together, all had been destroyed in Brian's orgy of despair and devastation. Even Mike's paintings had been slashed and thrown down. Anger and hatred filled her, but was swiftly gone. She had been right in what she had told the police: Brian had been driven to this extreme by Tina's behaviour. He just hadn't been strong enough to withstand it, that was all. She picked up an ornament, a cheap little rabbit that Mike had won at a fair long ago, and tried to put it back together with clumsy fingers, then gave up as tears came and she wept in despair, giving way at last to a grief that she had always kept tight inside her.

She sat there among the debris for a long time, desolately crying and thinking that she would have nothing of Mike left, but gradually realised that things didn't really matter because Mike's memory was safe in her heart where it would always be. And, as she sat there, so the pain of loss was healed as she found an inner peace and a sense of renewal. Her tears dried as Casey realised what she must do. She washed her face, dressed, and found some clothes which she packed into a bag, then she called a taxi and had it drive her round to Ivo's flat.

A church clock was striking three when Casey walked along the corridor to his flat. She pressed the bell, expecting him to take some time to answer, and was surprised when the door was opened almost at once. He was wearing a towelling robe, his feet and legs bare, but his hair was too tidy, his features too taut for him to have just awakened from sleep. When he saw her Ivo's face whitened, but was quickly drawn into an inscrutable mask, and he just stood there at the door, silent and unmoving.

She opened her mouth to tell him what had happened at the flat, but the words died as she looked into his eyes, so dark and wary. She said unsteadily, 'You once said that you wanted to sleep with me. To hold me.' Her eyes searched his face. 'I want that too, very much. So I—I came. Will you let me stay?' Her voice broke. 'I need you very badly tonight, Ivo.'

He gazed into her face for a long moment, his features like stone, but then he stepped back and let her in.

'Th-thank you.'

She waited until he had closed the door and then followed him into the sitting-room. She was right, he hadn't been in bed; the all-night television programme was on and there was a half-empty glass on a small table beside his armchair. He looked at her for a moment, then opened the door to the bedroom. 'You can sleep in there.'

Her chin came up, but her eyes were large in her pale face. 'I want to sleep with you.'

A quiver ran through him, and Ivo hesitated again before he switched off the television and the lights.

He closed the bedroom door behind them, leaned on it and said, 'What have you done to your face?'

'I'll tell you in the morning.' Putting down her bag, Casey began to undress, her fingers trembling.

Ivo watched her for a moment, his face taut with tension, then walked round to the other side of the bed, took off his robe, and slid between the covers. When she'd undressed, Casey sat on the edge of the bed with her back to him while she took off her watch and put it on the bedside-table. She grew still and, after a long moment, said, 'It's very hard to come to terms with grief and it takes a long time. You can face up to the big things like always being alone because you can anticipate and prepare yourself for them. But it's the little things that take you unawares, like not being able to repair a plug, or turning to share something good and finding no one there.'

She fell silent, but then felt Ivo's hand on her shoulder, warm and comforting. With a cry of gladness, Casey turned and went in beside him, let him put his arms round her and hold her. He didn't say anything, didn't ask any questions, just gently stroked her hair, overwhelmed to have her back in his arms but terrified of losing her again. Casey lay at peace in his embrace, her trust in him completely justified as he took care to control his own emotions. But after a while she smiled and raised herself on her elbow—then leaned over and kissed him, a kiss of passion and hunger and love.

Ivo slowly opened his eyes when she raised her head, and found her looking down at him. 'Do you know what you're doing?' he said in a kind of growl.

She nodded. 'Yes.'

He stared into her face. 'You're different. You're not afraid any more.'

'No.' And she kissed him a second time.

'If you do that again, I might find it very hard to keep my promise,' he warned her breathlessly.

'Then I'll just have to help you,' Casey informed him in loving mischief. 'Now, all you have to do is just lie back—and think of England.'

She ran her hand over him, lightly exploring, and began to kiss him, but it was only a few hot minutes before he gave a great moan and, grabbing hold of her, pulled her up beside him.

'To hell with England!' he said fiercely, and took the prize he so desperately wanted.

Harlequin Presents®

Coming Next Month

#1335 TOO STRONG TO DENY Emma Darcy
Elizabeth's principles lead her to ask Price Domenico, a top lawyer, to clear her of something she hasn't done. She needs his help no matter what it costs, though she hadn't reckoned on it costing her heart....

#1336 LOVE AT FIRST SIGHT Sandra Field
Bryden Moore is blind, but Casey Landrigan knows his real problem is his inability to love. Neither denies the growing attraction between them, but do they stand a chance when Bryden discovers Casey's true identity and the real reason she's vacationing next door?

#1337 WEB OF DESIRE Rachel Ford
The request to go to the Caribbean island of Halcyon Cay to restore valuable tapestries should have delighted Camilla. Instead it throws her into turmoil. For Halcyon Cay would have been *her* island if it weren't for Matthew Corrigan.

#1338 BITTER SECRET Carol Gregor
The charismatic new owner of Sedbury Hall is an unwelcome intrusion into Sophie's well-controlled world. She's instantly attracted to him—but determined to live her life alone....

#1339 TIME FOR TRUST Penny Jordan
The traumas of Jessica's past mean she can no longer trust anyone—not even her parents. Then she falls in love with and weds Daniel Hayward—but would love, without trust, survive?

#1340 LET FATE DECIDE Annabel Murray
It's easy for Jenni to believe that meeting Clay Cunningham's blue eyes across a crowded marketplace was meant to happen. But it's not so easy for Jenni to cope with her feelings once Clay makes it clear that any relationship between the two will be on his terms.

#1341 THE DEVIL'S EDEN Elizabeth Power
Coralie Rhodes—working under the name Lee Roman—desperately needs an interview with Jordan Colyer's famous uncle, to rescue her flagging magazine. But events of eight years ago had convinced Jordan that Coralie is a gold digger. Will he take his revenge now?

#1342 CONDITIONAL SURRENDER Wendy Prentice
Kate is shocked when Greg Courtney, her boss, reveals he's been burning with desire for her since their first meeting. Kate finds him attractive, too, but Greg is a cynic who doesn't believe in love. Kate is a romantic and knows that it's essential.

Available in February wherever paperback books are sold, or through Harlequin Reader Service:

In the U.S.
901 Fuhrmann Blvd.
P.O. Box 1397
Buffalo, N.Y. 14240-1397

In Canada
P.O. Box 603
Fort Erie, Ontario
L2A 5X3

HARLEQUIN'S "BIG WIN"
SWEEPSTAKES RULES & REGULATIONS
NO PURCHASE NECESSARY TO ENTER OR RECEIVE A PRIZE

1. To enter and join the Reader Service, scratch off the metallic strips on all your BIG WIN tickets #1-#6. This will reveal the values for each sweepstakes entry number, the number of free book(s) you will receive and your free bonus gift as part of our Reader Service. If you do not wish to take advantage of our Reader Service but wish to enter the Sweepstakes only, scratch off the metallic strips on your BIG WIN tickets #1-#4. Return your entire sheet of tickets intact. Incomplete and/or inaccurate entries are ineligible for that section or sections of prizes. Not responsible for mutilated or unreadable entries or inadvertent printing errors. Mechanically reproduced entries are null and void.

2. Whether you take advantage of this offer or not, your Sweepstakes numbers will be compared against the list of winning numbers generated at random by the computer. In the event that all prizes are not claimed by March 31, 1992, a random drawing will be held from all qualified entries received from March 30, 1990 to March 31, 1992, to award all unclaimed prizes. All cash prizes (Grand to Sixth), will be mailed to the winners and are payable by check in U.S. funds. Seventh Prize will be shipped to winners via third-class mail. These prizes are in addition to any free, surprise or mystery gifts that might be offered. Versions of this sweepstakes with different prizes of approximate equal value may appear at retail outlets or in other mailings by Torstar Corp. and its affiliates.

3. The following prizes are awarded in this sweepstakes: ★ Grand Prize (1) $1,000,000; First Prize (1) $25,000; Second Prize (1) $10,000; Third Prize (5) $5,000; Fourth Prize (10) $1,000; Fifth Prize (100) $250; Sixth Prize (2,500) $10; ★ ★ Seventh Prize (6,000) $12.95 ARV.

   ★ This presentation offers a Grand Prize of a $1,000,000 annuity. Winner will receive $33,333.33 a year for 30 years without interest totalling $1,000,000.

   ★ ★ Seventh Prize: A fully illustrated hardcover book published by Torstar Corp. Approximate retail value of the book is $12.95.

   Entrants may cancel the Reader Service at anytime without cost or obligation to buy (see details in center insert card).

4. This Sweepstakes is being conducted under the supervision of an independent judging organization. By entering this Sweepstakes, each entrant accepts and agrees to be bound by these rules and the decisions of the judges, which shall be final and binding. Odds of winning in the random drawing are dependent upon the total number of entries received. Taxes, if any, are the sole responsibility of the winners. Prizes are nontransferable. All entries must be received at the address printed on the reply card and must be postmarked no later than 12:00 MIDNIGHT on March 31, 1992. The drawing for all unclaimed sweepstakes prizes will take place May 30, 1992, at 12:00 NOON, at the offices of Marden-Kane, Inc., Lake Success, New York.

5. This offer is open to residents of the U.S., the United Kingdom, France and Canada, 18 years or older, except employees and their immediate family members of Torstar Corp., its affiliates, subsidiaries, and all other agencies and persons connected with the use, marketing or conduct of this sweepstakes. All Federal, State, Provincial and local laws apply. Void wherever prohibited or restricted by law. Any litigation within the Province of Quebec respecting the conduct and awarding of a prize in this publicity contest must be submitted to the Régie des loteries et courses du Québec.

6. Winners will be notified by mail and may be required to execute an affidavit of eligibility and release, which must be returned within 14 days after notification or an alternative winner will be selected. Canadian winners will be required to correctly answer an arithmetical skill-testing question administered by mail, which must be returned within a limited time. Winners consent to the use of their names, photographs and/or likenesses for advertising and publicity in conjunction with this and similar promotions without additional compensation. For a list of major winners, send a stamped, self-addressed envelope to: WINNERS LIST, c/o Harlequin Reader Service, 3010 Walden Ave., P.O. Box 1396, Buffalo, NY 14269-1396. Winners Lists will be fulfilled after the May 30, 1992 drawing date.

If Sweepstakes entry form is missing, please print your name and address on a 3" × 5" piece of plain paper and send to:

In the U.S.	In Canada
Harlequin's "BIG WIN" Sweepstakes	Harlequin's "BIG WIN" Sweepstakes
3010 Walden Ave.	P.O. Box 609
P.O. Box 1867	Fort Erie, Ontario
Buffalo, NY 14269-1867	L2A 5X3

Offer limited to one per household.

© 1991 Harlequin Enterprises Limited   Printed in the U.S.A.

LTY-H191R

Don't miss one exciting moment of you next vacation with Harlequin's

FREE
FIRST CLASS TRAVEL ALARM CLOCK

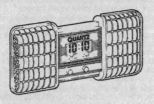

Actual Size
3¼″ × 1¼″h

By reading FIRST CLASS—Harlequin Romance's armchair travel plan for the incurably romantic— you'll not only visit a different dreamy destination every month, but you'll also receive a FREE TRAVEL ALARM CLOCK!

All you have to do is collect 2 proofs-of-purchase from FIRST CLASS Harlequin Romance books. FIRST CLASS is a one title per month series, available from January to December 1991.

For further details, see FIRST CLASS premium ads in FIRST CLASS Harlequin Romance books. Look for these books with the special FIRST CLASS cover flash!

JTLOOK